# THE COPPERHEAD

*AND OTHER STORIES*

**AMS PRESS**

**NEW YORK**

# THE COPPERHEAD

## *AND OTHER STORIES*

### *OF THE NORTH DURING THE AMERICAN WAR*

BY

## HAROLD FREDERIC

AUTHOR OF

"IN THE VALLEY," "THE RETURN OF THE O'MAHONY"
ETC.

LONDON

## WILLIAM HEINEMANN

1894

Reprinted from the edition of 1894, London
First AMS edition published in 1972
Manufactured in the United States of America

International Standard Book Number: 0-404-02571-4

Library of Congress Card Catalog Number: 70-144610


AMS PRESS, INC.
NEW YORK, N.Y. 10003

# DEDICATION

MY DEAR BRANDON THOMAS

Once upon a time—far too long ago, alas!—there were two little
boys, who had never heard of each other, and who lived
thousands of miles apart. While they were still young, a
terrible and protracted war was fought, and the men-folk
of the American boy's family went to it on the side of the
North and were killed. The father of the English lad,
though he had never been in America, set his heart on the
victory of the North, and had a flag of the Stars and
Stripes made for him, and kept it flying over his home in
Lancashire during that embittered and anxious time

Years afterward, these two urchins, now come to manhood, met
and were friends. To this day what they like best to talk
about, and what stands out most sharply in their minds,
is that boyhood time of theirs, when their alert eyes took
in all they saw, and their fresh hearts were keen to be
fluttered by heroic deeds and high enthusiasms

This book seeks to fix in type some of the pictures of that period
which stick in my recollection, and which, by comparison,
make all the later things blurred and indistinct. Such as
it is, I offer it to you, to help us to associate together in
the memories we prize so much, the Englishman who hung
out the flag and the Americans who died under it

Always all yours

HAROLD FREDERIC

# CONTENTS

# THE COPPERHEAD

# THE COPPERHEAD

## I

IT was on the night of my thirteenth birthday, I know, that the old farmhouse was burnt over our heads. By that reckoning I must have been six or seven when I went to live with Farmer Beech, because at the time he testified I had been with him half my life.

Abner Beech had often been supervisor for his town, and could have gone to the Assembly, it was said, had he chosen. He was a stalwart, thick-shouldered, big man, with shaggy dark eyebrows shading stern hazel eyes, and with a long, straight nose, and a broad, firmly-shut mouth. His expansive upper lip was blue from many years of shaving ; all the rest was bushing beard, mounting high upon the cheeks and rolling downward in iron-grey billows over his breast. That shaven upper lip, which still may be found among the farmers of the old blood in our district, was, I daresay, a survival from the time of the Puritan protest against the moustaches of the Cavaliers. If Abner Beech, in the latter days, had been told that this shaving on Wednesday and Saturday nights was a New England rite, I feel sure he would never have touched razor again.

He was a well-to-do man in the earlier time—a tremendous worker, a "good provider," a citizen of weight and substance in the community. In all large matters the neighbourhood looked to him to take the lead. He was the first farmer round about to set a mowing-machine to work in his meadows, and to put up lightning-rods on his buildings. At one period he was, too, the chief pillar in the church, but that was before the episode of the lightning-rods. Our little Union meeting-house was supplied in those days by an irregular procession of itinerant preachers, who came when the spirit moved, and spoke with that entire frankness which is induced by knowledge that the night is to be spent somewhere else. One of these strolling ministers regarded all attempts to protect property from lightning as an insolent defiance of the Divine Will, and said so very pointedly in the pulpit, and the congregation sat still and listened and grinned. Farmer Beech never forgave them.

There came in good time other causes for ill-

feeling. It is beyond the power of my memory
to pick out and arrange in proper sequence the
events which, in the final result, separated Abner
Beech from his fellows. My own recollections
go with distinctness back to the reception of the
news that Virginia had hanged John Brown ; in a
vaguer way they cover the two or three pre-
ceding years. Very likely Farmer Beech had
begun to fall out of touch with his neighbours
even before that.

The circumstances of my adoption into his
household—an orphan without relations or other
friends—were not of the sort to serve this narrative. I was taken in to be raised as a farm-hand,
and was no more expected to be grateful than as
if I had been a young steer purchased to toil in
the yoke. No suggestion was ever made that
I had incurred any debt of obligation to the
Beeches. In a little community where every one
worked as a matter of course till there was no
more work to do, and all shared alike the simple
food, the tired, heavy sleep, and the infrequent
spells of recreation, no one talked or thought of
benefits conferred or received. My rights in the
house and about the place were neither less nor
more than those of Jeff Beech, the farmer's only
son.

In the course of time I came, indeed, to be a
more sympathetic unit in the household, so to

speak, than poor Jeff himself. But that was only because he had been drawn off after strange gods.

At all times—even when nothing else good was said of him—Abner Beech was spoken of by the people of the district as a "great hand for reading." His pre-eminence in this matter remained unquestioned to the end. No other farmer for miles owned half the number of books which he had on the shelves above his writing-desk. Still less was there any one round about who could for a moment stand up with him in a discussion involving book-learning in general. This at first secured for him the respect of the whole country-side, and men were proud to be agreed with by such a scholar. But when affairs changed, this, oddly enough, became a formidable popular grievance against Abner Beech. They said then that his opinions were worthless because he got them from printed books, instead of from his heart.

What these opinions were may in some measure be guessed from the titles of the farmer's books. Perhaps there were as many as thirty of them behind the glass doors of the old mahogany book-case. With one or two agricultural or veterinary exceptions, they related exclusively to American history and politics. There were, I recall, the first two volumes of Bancroft, and Lossing's "Lives of the Signers," and "Field Books" of the two wars

with England ; Thomas H. Benton's " Thirty
Years' View"; the four green-black volumes of
Hammond's " Political History of the State of
New York"; campaign lives of Lewis Cass and
Franklin Pierce, and larger biographies of
Jefferson and Jackson, and, most imposing of
all, a whole long row of big calf-bound volumes of
the *Congressional Globe*, which carried the minutiæ
of politics at Washington back into the forties.

These books constituted the entire literary side
of my boyish education. I have only the faintest
and haziest recollections of what happened when I
went during the winter months to the school-house
at the Four Corners. But I can recall the very
form of the type in the farmer's books. Every
one of those quaint, austere, and beardless faces,
framed in high collars and stocks and waving hair
—the Marcys, Calhouns, De Witt Clintons, and
Silas Wrights of the daguerreotype and Sartain's
primitive graver—gives back to me now the
lineaments of an old-time friend.

Whenever I could with decency escape from
playing checkers with Jeff, and had no harness to
grease or other indoor jobs, I spent the winter
evenings in poring over some one of these books—
generally with Abner Beech at the opposite side
of the table immersed in another. On some rare
occasion one of the hired men would take down
a volume and look through it—the farmer watch-

ing him covertly the while to see that he did not wet his big thumbs to turn over the leaves—but for the most part we two had the books to ourselves. The others would sit about till bedtime, amusing themselves as best they could, the women-folk knitting or mending, the men cracking butternuts, or dallying with cider and apples and fried cakes, as they talked over the work and gossip of the district and tempted the scorching impulses of the stove-hearth with their stockinged feet.

This tacit separation of the farmer and myself from the rest of the household in the course of time begat confidences between us. He grew, from brief and casual beginnings, into a habit of speaking to me about the things we read. As it became apparent, year by year, that young Jeff was never going to read anything at all, Abner Beech more and more distinguished me with conversational favour. It cannot be said that the favouritism showed itself in other directions. I had to work as hard as ever, and got no more playtime than before. The master's eye was everywhere, as keen, alert, and unsparing as if I had not known even my alphabet. But when there were breathing spells, we talked together— or rather he talked and I listened—as if we were folk quite apart from the rest.

Two fixed ideas thus arose in my boyish mind, and dominated all my little notions of the world.

One was that Alexander Hamilton and John
Marshall were among the most infamous characters
in history. The other was that every true
American ought to hold himself in daily readiness
to fight with England. I gave a great deal of
thought to both these matters. I had early con-
victions, too, I remember, with regard to Daniel
Webster, who had been very bad, and then all at
once became a very good man. For some obscure
reason I always connected him in my imagination with Zaccheus up a tree, and clung to the
queer association of images long after I learned
that the Marshfield statesman had been physically
a large man.

Gradually the old blood-feud with the Britisher
became obscured by fresher antagonisms, and
there sprouted up a crop of new sons of Belial who
deserved to be hated more even than had
Hamilton and Marshall. With me the two
stages of indignation glided into one another so
imperceptibly that I can now hardly distinguish
between them. What I do recall is that the
farmer came in time to neglect the hereditary
enemy, England, and to seem to have quite forgotten our own historic foes to liberty, so enraged
was he over the modern Abolitionists. He told
me about them as we paced up the seed-rows together in the spring, as we drove homeward on the
hay-load in the cool of the summer evening, as we

shovelled out a path for the women to the pump in the farmyard through December snows. It took me a long time to even approximately grasp the wickedness of these new men, who desired to establish negro sovereignty in the Republic, and to compel each white girl to marry a black man.

The mere fact that I had never seen any negro "close to," and had indeed only caught passing glimpses of one or more of the coloured race on the streets of our nearest big town, added, no doubt, to the mystified alarm with which I contemplated these monstrous proposals. When finally an old darky on his travels did stroll our way, and I beheld him, incredibly ragged, dirty and light-hearted, shuffling through "Jump Jim Crow" down at the Four Corners, for the ribald delectation of the village loafers, the revelation fairly made me shudder. I marvelled that the others could laugh, with this unspeakable fate hanging over their silly heads.

At first the Abolitionists were to me a remote and intangible class, who lived and wrought their evil deeds in distant places—chiefly New England way. I rarely heard mention of any names of persons among them. They seemed to be an impersonal mass, like a herd of buffaloes or a swarm of hornets. The first individuality in their ranks which attracted my attention, I remember, was that of Theodore Parker. The farmer one day brought home with him from town a pamphlet composed of anti-slavery sermons or addresses by this person. In the evening he read it, or as far into it as his temper would permit, beating the table with his huge fist from time to time, and snorting with wrathful amazement. At last he sprang to his feet, marched over to the wood-stove, kicked the door open with his boot, and thrust the offending print into the blaze. It is vivid in my memory still—the way the red flame-light flared over his big burly front, and sparkled on his beard, and made his face to shine like that of Moses.

But soon I learned that there were Aboli-tionists everywhere—Abolitionists right here in our own little farmland township of northern New York! The impression which this discovery made upon me was not unlike that produced on Robinson Crusoe by the immortal footprint. I could think of nothing else. Great events, which really covered a space of years, came and went as in a bunch together, while I was still pondering upon this. John Brown was hanged, Lincoln was elected, Sumter was fired on, the first regiment was raised and despatched from our rustic end of Dearborn County—and all the time it seems now as if my mind was concentrated upon the amazing fact that some of our neighbours were Abolitionists!

There was a certain dreamlike tricksiness of transformation in it all. At first there was only one Abolitionist, old " Jee " Hagadorn. Then, somehow, there came to be a number of them— and then, all at once, lo ! everybody was an Abolitionist—that is to say, everybody but Abner Beech. The more general and enthusiastic the conversion of the others became, the more resolutely and doggedly he dug his heels into the ground, and braced his broad shoulders, and pulled in the opposite direction. The skies darkened, the wind rose, the storm of angry popular feeling burst swooping over the countryside, but Beech only stiffened his back and never budged an inch.

At some early stage of this great change we ceased going to church at all. The pulpit of our rustic meeting-house had become a platform from which the farmer found himself denounced with hopeless regularity on every recurring Sabbath, and that, too, without any chance whatever of talking back. This in itself was hardly to be borne. But when others, mere laymen of the church, took up the theme, and began in class-meetings and the Sunday-school to talk about Antichrist and the Beast with Ten Horns and Seven Heads, in obvious connection with Southern sympathisers, it became frankly insufferable. The farmer did not give in without a fierce resistance.

He collected all the texts he could find in the Bible, such as "Servants obey your masters," "Cursed be Canaan," and the like, and hurled them vehemently, with strong, deep voice and sternly glowing eyes, full at their heads. But the others had many more texts—we learned afterwards that old "Jee" Hagadorn enjoyed the unfair advantage of a Cruden's Concordance— and their tongues were as forty to one, so we left off going to church altogether.

Not long after this, I should think, came the miserable affair of the cheese-factory.

The idea of doing all the dairy work of a neighbourhood under a common roof, which originated not many miles from us, was now nearly ten years old. In those days it was regarded as having in it possibilities of vastly greater things than mere cheese-making. Its success among us had stirred up in men's minds big sanguine notions of co-operation as the answer to all American farm-problems—as the gateway through which we were to march into the rural millennium. These high hopes one recalls now with a smile and a sigh. Farmers' wives continued to break down and die under the strain, or to be drafted off to the lunatic asylums ; the farmers kept on hanging themselves in their barns, or flying westward before the locust-like cloud of mortgages ; the boys and girls turned their steps townward in an ever-increasing host. The millennium never came at all.

But at that time—in the late fifties and early sixties—the cheese-factory was the centre of an impressive constellation of dreams and roseate promises. Its managers were the very elect of the district ; their disfavour was more to be dreaded than any condemnation of a town-meeting ; their chief officers were even more important personages than the supervisor and assessor.

Abner Beech had literally been the founder of our cheese-factory. I fancy he gave the very land on which it was built, and where you will see it still, under the willows by the upper-creek bridge. He sent to it in those days the milk of the biggest herd owned by any farmer for miles around, reaching at seasons nearly one hundred cows. His voice, too, outweighed all others in its co-operative councils.

But when our church-going community had reached the conclusion that a man couldn't be a Christian and hold such views on the slave question as Beech held, it was only a very short step to the conviction that such a man would water his milk. In some parts of the world the theft of a horse is the most heinous of conceivable crimes ; other sections exalt to this pinnacle of sacredness in property a sheep, or a pheasant, or a woman.

Among our dairymen the thing of special sanctity was milk. A man in our neighbourhood might almost better be accused of forgery or bigamy outright, than to fall under the dreadful suspicion of putting water into his cans.

Whether it was mere stupid prejudice or malignant invention I know not—who started the story was never to be learned—but of a sudden everybody seemed to have heard that Abner Beech's milk had been refused at the cheese-factory. This was not true, any more than it was true that there could possibly have been warrant for such a proceeding. But what did happen was that the cheese-maker took elaborate pains each morning to test our cans with such primitive appliances as preceded the lactometer, and sniffed suspiciously as he entered our figures in a separate book, and behaved generally so that our hired man knocked him head over heels into one of his whey vats. Then the managers complained to the farmer. He went down to meet them, boiling over with rage. There was an evil spirit in the air, and bitter words were exchanged. The outcome was that Abner Beech renounced the co-operative curds of his earlier manhood, so to speak, sold part of his cattle at a heavy loss, and began making butter at home with the milk of the remainder.

Then we became pariahs in good earnest.

## II

THE farmer came in from the fields somewhat earlier than usual on this August afternoon. He walked, I remember, with a heavy step and bowed head, and when he had come into the shade on the porch and taken off his hat, looked about him with a wearied air. The great heat, with its motionless atmosphere and sultry closeness, had well-nigh wilted everybody. But one could see that Abner was suffering more than the rest, and from something beyond the enervation of dog-days.

He sank weightily into the armchair by the desk, and stretched out his legs with a querulous note in his accustomed grunt of relief. On the moment Mrs. Beech came in from the kitchen, with the big china wash-bowl filled with cold water, and the towel and clean socks over her arm, and knelt before her husband. She proceeded to pull off his big, dust-baked boots and the woollen foot-gear, put his feet into the bowl, bathe and dry them, and draw on the fresh covering, all without a word.

The ceremony was one I had watched many hundreds of times. Mrs. Beech was a tall, dark, silent woman, whom I could well believe to have been handsome in her youth. She belonged to one of the old Mohawk-Dutch families, and when some of her sisters came to visit at the farm I noted that they, too, were all dusky as squaws, with jet-black shiny curls and eyes like the midnight hawk. I used always to be afraid of them on this account, but I daresay they were in reality most kindly women. Mrs. Beech herself represented to my boyish eyes the ideal of a saturnine and masterful queen. She performed great quantities of work with no apparent effort —as if she had merely willed it to be done. Her household was governed with a cold impassive exactitude ; there were never any hitches, or even high words. The hired-girls, of course, called her " M'rye," as the rest of us mostly did, but they rarely carried familiarity farther, and as a rule respected her dislike for much talk. During all the years I spent under her roof I was never clear in my mind as to whether she liked me or not. Her own son, even, passed his boyhood in much the same state of dubiety.

But to her husband, Abner Beech, she was always most affectionately docile and humble. Her snapping black eyes followed him about and rested on him with an almost canine fidelity of liking. She spoke to him habitually in a voice quite different from that which others heard addressed to them. This, indeed, was measurably

B

true of us all. By instinct the whole household deferred in tone and manner to our big, bearded chief, as if he were an Arab sheik ruling over us in a tent on the desert. The word " patriarch " still seems best to describe him, and his attitude towards us and the world in general, as I recall him sitting there in the half-darkened living-room, with his wife bending over his feet in true Oriental submission.

" Do you know where Jeff is ? " the farmer suddenly asked, without turning his head to where I sat braiding a whip-lash, but indicating by the volume of voice that his query was put to me.

" He went off about two o'clock," I replied, " with his fish-pole.   They say they are biting like everything down in the creek."

" Well, you keep to work and they won't bite you," said Abner Beech.   This was a very old joke with him, and usually the opportunity of using it once more tended to lighten his mood. Now, though mere force of habit led him to repeat the pleasantry, he had no pleasure in it.   He sat with his head bent, and his huge hairy hands spread listlessly on the chair-arms.

Mrs. Beech finished her task, and rose, lifting the bowl from the floor.   She paused, and looked wistfully into her husband's face.

" You ain't a bit well, Abner ! " she said.

"Well as I'm likely ever to be again," he made answer, gloomily.

"Has any more of 'em been sayin' or doin' anything?" the wife asked, with diffident hesitation.

The farmer spoke with more animation. "D'ye suppose I care a picayune what *they* say or do?" he demanded. "Not I! But when a man's own kith and kin turn agin him, into the bargain——" he left the sentence unfinished, and shook his head to indicate the impossibility of such a situation.

"Has Jeff—then——" Mrs. Beech began to ask.

"Yes—Jeff!" thundered the farmer, striking his fist on the arm of the chair. "Yes—by the Eternal!—Jeff!"

When Abner Beech swore by the Eternal we knew that things were pretty bad. His wife put the bowl down on a chair, and seated herself in another. "What's Jeff been doin'?" she asked.

"Why, where do you suppose he was last night, and the night before that? Where do you suppose he is this minute? They ain't no mistake about it. Lee Watkins saw 'em with his own eyes, and ta'nted me with it. He's down by the red bridge—that's where he is—hangin' round that Hagadorn gal!"

Mrs. Beech looked properly aghast at the intelligence. Even to me it was apparent that the unhappy Jeff might better have been

employed in committing any other crime under
the sun.  It was only to be expected that his
mother would be horrified.

"I never could abide that Lee Watkins," was
what she said.

The farmer did not comment on the relevancy
of this.

"Yes," he went on, "the daughter of mine
enemy, the child of that whining, backbiting old
scoundrel who's been eating his way into me like
a deer-tick for years—the whelp that I owe every
mean and miserable thing that's ever happened to
me—yes, of all living human creatures, by the
Eternal! it's *his* daughter that that blamed fool
of a Jeff must take a shine to, and hang around
after!"

"He'll come of age the fourteenth of next
month," remarked the mother, tentatively.

"Yes—and march up and vote the Woolly-
head ticket.  I suppose that's what'll come
next!" said the farmer, bitterly.  "It only needed
that!"

"And it was you who got her the job of teachin'
the school, too," put in Mrs. Beech.

"That's nothing to do with it," Abner continued.
"I ain't blaming her—that is, on her own account.
She's a good enough gal so far's I know.  But
everything and everybody under that tumble-
down Hagadorn roof ought to be pizen to any

son of mine! *That's* what I say! And I tell
you this, mother"—the farmer rose, and spread
his broad chest, towering over the seated woman
as he spoke—" I tell you this ; if he ain't got
pride enough to keep him away from that house
—away from that gal—then he can keep away
from *this* house—away from me ! "

The wife looked up at him mutely, then bowed
her head in tacit consent.

" He brings it on himself ! " Abner cried, with
clenched fists, beginning to pace up and down the
room. " Who's the one man I've reason to curse
with my dying breath ? Who began the infernal
Abolition cackle here ? Who drove me out of
the church ? Who started that outrageous lie
about the milk at the factory, and chased me out
of that, too ? Who's been a layin' for years
behind every stump and every bush, waitin' for
the chance to stab me in the back, an' ruin my
business, an' set my neighbours agin me, an' land
me an' mine in the poorhouse or the lock-up ?
You know as well as I do—' Jee ' Hagadorn !
If I'd wrung his scrawny little neck for him the
first time I ever laid eyes on him, it would have
been money in my pocket and years added onto
my life. And then my son—*my* son ! must go
taggin' around—oh-h ! "

He ended with an inarticulate growl of impa-
tience·and wrath.

" Mebbe, if you spoke to the boy——" Mrs. Beech began.

" Yes, I'll speak to him ! " the farmer burst forth, with grim emphasis. "I'll speak to him so't he'll hear." He turned abruptly to me. " Here, boy," he said, " you go down the creek-road an' look for Jeff. If he ain't loafing round the school-house he'll be in the neighbourhood of Hagadorn's. You tell him I say for him to get back here as quick as he can." You needn't tell him what it's about. Pick up your feet, now."

As luck would have it, I had scarcely got out to the road before I heard the loose-spoked wheels of the local butcher's waggon rattling behind me down the hill. Looking round, I saw through the accompanying puffs of dust that young " Ni " Hagadorn was driving, and that he was alone. I stopped and waited for him to come up, questioning my mind whether it would be fair to beg a lift from him when the purpose of my journey was so hostile to his family. Even after he had halted, and I had climbed up to the seat beside him, this consciousness of treachery disturbed me.

But no one thought long of being serious with " Ni." He was along in the teens somewhere, not large for his years but extremely wiry and muscular, and the funniest boy any of us ever knew of. How the son of such a sad-faced, gloomy, old licensed exhorter as " Jee " Hagadorn

could be such a running spring of jokes and odd
sayings and general deviltry as " Ni," passed all
our understandings.    His very face made you
laugh, with its wilderness of freckles, its snub
nose, and the comical curl to its mouth.    He
must have been a profitable investment to the
butcher who hired him to drive about the country.
The farmers' wives all came out to laugh and
chat with him, and under the influence of his
good spirits they went on buying the toughest
steaks and bull-beef flanks, at more than city
prices, year after year.    But anybody who
thought " Ni " was soft because he was full of fun
made a great mistake.

" I see you ain't doing much ditching this
year," " Ni " remarked, glancing over our fields as
he started up the horse.    " I should think you'd
be tickled to death."

Well, in one sense I was glad.    There used to
be no other such back-aching work in all the
year as that picking up of stones to fill into the
trenches which the hired men began digging as
soon as the hay and grain were in.    But on the
other hand, I knew that the present idleness
meant—as everything else now seemed to mean—
that the Beech farm was going to the dogs.

" No," I made rueful answer.    " Our land don't
need draining any more.    It's dry as a powder-
horn now."

"Ni" clucked knowingly at the old horse. "Guess it's Abner that can't stand much more draining," he said. "They say he's looking all round for a mortgage, and can't raise one."

"No such thing!" I replied. "His health's poorly this summer, that's all. And Jeff—he don't seem to take hold, somehow, like he used to."

My companion laughed outright.

"Mustn't call him Jeff any more," he remarked, with a grin. "He was telling us down at the house that he was going to have people call him Tom after this. He can't stand answering to the same name as Jeff Davis," he says.

"I suppose you folks put him up to that," I made bold to comment indignantly.

The suggestion did not annoy "Ni." "Mebbe so," he said. "You know Dad lots a good deal on names. He's downright mortified that I don't get up and kill people because my name's Benaiah. 'Why,' he keeps on saying to me, 'Here you are, Benaiah, the son of Jehoiada, as it was in Holy Writ, and instead of preparin' to make ready to go out and fall on the enemies of righteousness, like your namesake did, all you do is read dime novels and cut up monkey-shines generally, for all the world as if you'd been named Pete or Steve or William Henry.' That's what he gives me pretty nearly every day."

companion obligingly drew up to let me get down. He called out some merry quip or other as he drove off, framed in a haze of golden dust against the sinking sun, and I stood looking after him with the pleasantest thoughts my mind had known for days. It was almost a shock to remember that he was one of the abhorrent and hated Hagadorns.

And his sister, too. It was not at all easy to keep one's loathing up to the proper pitch where so nice a girl as Esther Hagadorn was its object She was years and years my senior—she was even older than "Ni"—and had been my teacher for the past two winters. She had never spoken to me save across that yawning gulf which separates little bare-footed urchins from tall young women, with long dresses and their hair done up in a net, and I could hardly be said to know her at all. Yet now, perversely enough, I could think of nothing but her manifest superiority to all the farm-girls round about. She had been to a school in some remote city, where she had relations. Her hands were fabulously white, and even on the hottest of days her dresses rustled pleasantly with starched primness. People talked about her singing at church as something remarkable; to my mind, the real music was when she just spoke to you, even if it was no more than "Good morning, Jimmy!"

I was familiar enough with the quaint my
cism which the old Abolitionist cooper wove arou.
the Scriptural names of himself and his son. W
understood that these two appellations had alter-
nated among his ancestors as well, and I had
often heard him read from Samuel and Kings and
Chronicles about them, his stiff red hair standing
upright, and the blue veins swelling on his narrow
temples with proud excitement. But that, of
course, was in the old days, before the trouble
came, and when I still went to church. To hear
it all now again seemed to give me a novel impression of wild fanaticism in " Jee " Hagadorn.

His son was chuckling on his seat over something he had just remembered. " Last time," he
began, gurgling with laughter—" last time he went
for me because I wasn't measuring up to his idee
of what a Benaiah ought to be like, I up and said
to him, 'Look a-here now, people who live in
glass houses mustn't heave rocks. If I'm Benaiah
you're Jehoiada. Well, it says in the Bible that
Jehoiada made a cove-nant. Do you make cove-
nants ? Not a bit of it ! all you make is butter
firkins, with now and then an odd pork barrel.' "

" What did he say to that ? " I asked, as my
companion's merriment abated.

" Well, I come away just then ; I seemed to
have business outside," replied " Ni," still grinning.

We had reached the Corners now, and my

I clambered up on the window-sill of the school-house, to make sure there was no one inside, and then set off down the creek-road toward the red or lower bridge. Milking-time was about over, and one or two teams passed me on the way to the cheese-factory, the handles of the cans rattling as they went, and the low sun throwing huge shadows of drivers and horses sprawling eastward over the stubble-field. I cut across lots to avoid the cheese-factory itself, with some vague feeling that it was not a fitting spectacle for any one who lived on the Beech farm.

A few moments brought me to the bank of the wandering stream below the factory, but so near that I could hear the creaking of the chain drawing up the cans over the tackle, or, as we called it, the "teekle." The willows under which I walked stretched without a break from the clump by the factory bridge. And now, lo and behold! beneath still other of these willows, farther down the stream, whom should I see strolling together, but my school-teacher and the delinquent Jeff!

Young Beech bore still the fish-pole I had seen him take from our shed some hours earlier, but the line twisted round it was very white and dry. He was extremely close to the girl, and kept his head bent down over her as they sauntered along the meadow-path. They seemed not to be talk-ing, but just idly drifting forward like the deep slow water beside them. I had never realised before how tall Jeff was. Though the school-ma'am always seemed to me of an exceeding stature, here was Jeff rounding his shoulders and inclining his neck in order to look under her broad-brimmed Leghorn hat.

There could be no imaginable excuse for my not overtaking them. Instinct prompted me to start up a whistling tune as I advanced—a casual and indolently unobtrusive tune—at sound of which Jeff straightened himself, and gave his companion a little more room on the path. In a moment or two he stopped, and looked intently over the bank into the water, as if he hoped it might turn out to be a likely place for fish. And the school-ma'am, too, after a few aimless steps, halted to help him look.

" Abner wants you to come right straight home! " was the form in which my message delivered itself when I had come close up to them.

They both shifted their gaze from the sluggish stream below to me upon the instant. Then Esther Hagadorn looked away, but Jeff—good, big, honest Jeff, who had been like a fond elder brother to me since I could remember—knitted his brows and regarded me with something like a scowl.

" Did pa send you to say that ? " he demanded,

holding my eye with a glance of such stern inquiry that I could only nod my head in confusion.

"And he knew that you'd find me here, did
he?"

"He said either at the school-house or around
here somewhere," I admitted, weakly.

"And there ain't nothing the matter at the
farm? He don't want me for nothing special?"
pursued Jeff, still looking me through and through.

"He didn't say," I made hesitating answer; but
for the life of me, I could not keep from throwing
a tell-tale look in the direction of his companion
in the blue gingham dress.

A wink could not have told Jeff more. He
gave a little bitter laugh, and stared above my
head at the willow-plumes for a minute's meditation, Then he tossed his fish-pole over to me
and laughed again.

"Keep that for yourself, if you want it," he
said, in a voice not quite his own, but robustly
enough. "I sha'n't need it any more. Tell pa
I ain't a-coming!"

"Oh, Tom!" Esther broke in, anxiously,
"would you do that?"

He held up his hand with a quiet, masterful
gesture, as if she were the pupil and he the
teacher. "Tell him," he went on, the tone falling
now strong and true, "tell him and ma that I'm
going to Tecumseh to-night to enlist. If they're

willing to say good-bye, they can let me know there, and I'll manage to slip back for the day. If they ain't willing—why, they—they needn't send word ; that's all."

Esther had come up to him, and held his arm now in hers.

"You're wrong to leave them like that !" she pleaded, earnestly, but Jeff shook his head.

"You don't know him !" was all he said.

In another minute I had shaken hands with Jeff, and had started on my homeward way, with his parting, " Good-bye, youngster !" benumbing my ears.   When, after a while, I turned to look back, they were still standing where I had left them, gazing over the bank into the water.

Then, as I trudged onward once more, I began to quake at the thought of how Farmer Beech would take the news.


## III


ONCE, in the duck-season, as I lay hidden among the marsh-reeds with an older boy, a crow passed over us, flying low.   Looking up at him, I realised for the first time how beautiful a creature was this common black thief of ours—how splendid his strength and the sheen of his coat, how proudly graceful the sweep and curves of his great slow wings. The boy beside me fired, and in a flash what I had been admiring changed— even as it stopped headlong in mid-air—into a hideous thing, an evil confusion of jumbled feathers. The awful swiftness of that transition from beauty and power to hateful carrion haunted me for a long time.

I half expected that Abner Beech would crumple up in some such distressing way, all of a sudden, when I told him that his son Jeff was in open rebellion, and intended to go off and enlist. It was incredible to the senses that any member of the household should set at defiance the pa- triarchal will of its head. But that the offence should come from placid, slow-witted, good- natured Jeff, and that it should involve the ap- pearance of a Beech in a blue uniform—these things staggered the imagination. It was clear that something prodigious must happen.

As it turned out, nothing happened at all. The farmer and his wife sat out on the veranda, as was their wont of a summer evening, rarely exchanging a word, but getting a restful sort of satisfation in together surveying their barns and haystacks and the yellow-brown stretch of fields beyond.

" Jeff says he's going to-night to Tecumseh, and he's going to enlist, and if you want him to run over to say good-bye you're to let him know there."

I leant upon my newly-acquired fishpole for
support, as I unburdened myself of these sinister
tidings.   The old pair looked at me in calm-
eyed silence, as if I had related the most trivial of
village occurrences.   Neither moved a muscle nor
uttered a sound, but just gazed, till it felt as if
their eyes were burning holes into me.

" That's what he said," I repeated, after a
pause, to mitigate the embarrassment of that dumb
steadfast stare.

The mother it was who spoke at last.   " You'd
better go round and get your supper," she said
quietly.

The table was spread, as usual, in the big, low-
ceilinged room which during the winter was used
as a kitchen.   What was unusual was to discover a
strange man seated alone in his shirt sleeves at
this table, eating his supper.   As I took my chair,
however, I saw that he was not altogether a
stranger.   I recognised in him the little old
Irishman who had farmed Ezra Tracy's beaver
meadow the previous year on shares, and done
badly, and had since been hiring out for odd jobs
at hoeing and haying.   He had lately lost his
wife, I recalled now, and lived alone in a tumble-
down old shanty beyond Parker's saw-mill.   He
had come to us in the spring, I remembered, when
the brindled calf was born, to beg a pail of what he
called " basteings," and I speculated in my mind

whether it was this repellent mess that had killed
his wife. Above all these thoughts rose the
impression that Abner must have decided to do a
heap of ditching and wall-building, to have hired
a new hand in this otherwise slack season—and at
this my back began to ache prophetically.

" How are yeh ? " the new-comer remarked,
affably, as I sat down and reached for the bread.
" An' did yeh see the boys march away ?   An
had they a drum wid 'em ? "

" What boys ? " I asked, in blank ignorance as
to what he was at.

" I'm told there's a baker's dozen of 'em gone,
more or less," he replied.   " Well, glory be to the
Lord, 'tis an ill wind blows nobody good.   Here
am I aitin' butter on my bread, an' cheese on top
o' that."

I should still have been in the dark, had not
one of the hired girls, Janey Wilcox, come in
from the butter-room, to ask me in turn much
the same thing, and to add the explanation that
a whole lot of the young men of the neighbourhood had privately arranged among themselves to
enlist together as soon as the harvesting was over,
and had this day gone off in a body.   Among
them, I learned now, were our two hired men,
Warner Pitts and Ray Watkins.   This, then,
accounted for the presence of the Irishman.

As a matter of fact, there had been no secrecy

C

about the thing save with the contingent which our household furnished, and that was only because of the fear which Abner Beech inspired. His son and his servants alike preferred to hook it, rather than explain their patriotic impulses to him.　But, naturally enough, our farm-girls took it for granted that all the others had gone in the same surreptitious fashion, and this threw an air of fascinating mystery about the whole occurrence. They were deeply surprised that I should have been down past the Corners, and even beyond the cheese factory, and seen nothing of these extraordinary martial preparations ; and I myself was ashamed of it.

Opinions differed, I remember, as to the behaviour of our two hired men.　"Till" Babcock and the Underwood girl defended them, but Janey took the other side, not without various unpleasant personal insinuations, and the Irishman and I were outspoken in their condemnation.　But nobody said a word about Jeff, though it was plain enough that every one knew.

Dusk fell while we still talked of these astounding events — my thoughts meantime dividing themselves between efforts to realise these neighbours of ours as soldiers on the tented field, and uneasy speculation as to whether I should at last get a bed to myself or be expected to sleep with the Irishman.

Janey Wilcox had taken the lamp into the living-room. She returned now, with an uplifted hand and a face covered over with lines of surprise.

" You're to all of you come in," she whispered, impressively. " Abner's got the Bible down. We're going to have fam'ly prayers, or somethin'."

With one accord we looked at the Irishman. The question had never before arisen on our farm, but we all knew about other cases, in which Catholic hands held aloof from the household's devotions. There were even stories of their refusal to eat meat on some one day of the week, but this we hardly brought ourselves to credit. Our surprise at the fact that domestic religious observances were to be resumed under the Beech roof-tree—where they had completely lapsed ever since the trouble at the church—was as nothing compared with our curiosity to see what the new-comer would do.

What he did was to get up and come along with the rest of us, quite as a matter of course. I felt sure that he could not have understood what was going on.

We filed into the living-room. The Beeches had come in and shut the veranda door, and " M'rye " was seated in her rocking-chair, in the darkness beyond the bookcase. Her husband had the big book open before him on the table ;

the lamplight threw the shadow of his long nose down into the grey of his beard with a strange effect of fierceness. His lips were tight-set and his shaggy brows drawn into a commanding frown, as he bent over the pages.

Abner did not look up till we had taken our seats. Then he raised his eyes towards the Irishman.

"I don't know, Hurley," he said, in a grave, deep-booming voice, "whether you feel it right for you to join us—we being Protestants——"

"Ah, it's all right, sir," replied Hurley, re-assuringly, "I'll take no harm by it."

A minute's silence followed upon this magnanimous declaration. Then Abner, clearing his throat, began solemnly to read the story of Absalom's revolt. He had the knack, not uncommon in those primitive class-meeting days, of making his strong, low-pitched voice quaver and wail in the most tear-compelling fashion when he read from the Old Testament. You could hardly listen to him going through even the genealogical tables of Chronicles dry-eyed. His Jeremiah and Ezekiel were equal to the funeral of a well-beloved relation.

This night he read as I had never heard him read before. The whole grim story of the son's treason and final misadventure, of the ferocious battle in the wood of Ephraim, of Joab's savagery,

and of the rival runners, made the air vibrate
about us, and took possession of our minds and
kneaded them like dough, as we sat in the mute
circle in the old living-room. From my chair I
could see Hurley without turning my head, and
the spectacle of excitement he presented—bending forward with dropped jaw and wild, glistening
grey eyes, a hand behind his ear to miss no
syllable of this strange new tale—only added to
the effect it produced on me.

Then there came the terrible picture of the
King's despair. I had trembled as we neared
this part, foreseeing what heart-wringing anguish
Abner, in his present mood, would give to that
cry of the stricken father—" O my son Absalom,
my son, my son Absalom ! Would God I had
died for thee, O Absalom, my son, my son ! "
To my great surprise, he made very little of it.
The words came coldly, almost contemptuously,
so that the listener could not but feel that David's
lamentations were out of place, and might better
have been left unuttered.

But now the farmer, leaping over into the next
chapter, brought swart, stalwart, blood-stained
Joab on the scene before us, and in an instant we
saw why the King's outburst of mourning had
fallen so flat upon our ears. Abner Beech's voice
rose and filled the room with its passionate fervour
as he read out Joab's speech—wherein the King

is roundly told that his son was a worthless fellow, and was killed not a bit too soon, and that for the father to thus publicly lament him is to put to shame all his household and his loyal friends and servants.

While these sonorous words of protest against paternal weakness still rang in the air, Abner abruptly closed the book with a snap. We looked at him and at one another for a bewildered moment, and then "Till" Babcock stooped as if to kneel by her chair, but Janey nudged her, and we all rose and made our way silently out again into the kitchen. It had been apparent enough that no spirit of prayer abode in the farmer's breast.

"'Twas a fine, bold, sinsible man, that Job!" remarked Hurley to me, when the door was closed behind us, and the women had gone off to talk the scene over among themselves in the butter-room. "Would it be him that had thim lean turkeys?"

With some difficulty I made out his meaning. "Oh, no!" I explained, "the man Abner read about was Jo-ab, not Job. They were quite different people."

"I thought as much," replied the Irishman. "'Twould not be in so grand a man's nature to let his fowls go hungry. And do we be hearing such tales every night?"

" Maybe Abner 'll keep on, now he's started again," I said. " We ain't had any Bible-reading before since he had his row down at the church, and we left off going."

Hurley displayed such a lively interest in this matter that I went over it pretty fully, setting forth Abner's position and the intolerable provocations which had been forced upon him. It took him a long time to grasp the idea that in Protestant gatherings, not only the pastor spoke, but the class-leaders and all others who were conscious of a call might have their word as well, and that in this way even the lowliest and meanest of the farmer's neighbours had been able to affront him in the church itself.

"Too many cooks spoil the broth," was his comment upon this. "'Tis far better to hearken to one man only. If he's right, you're right. If he's wrong, why, thin, there ye have him in front of ye for protection."

Bedtime came soon after, and Mrs. Beech appeared in her nightly round of the house to see that the doors were all fastened. The candle she bore threw up a flaring yellow light upon her chin, but made the face above it by contrast still darker and more saturnine. She moved about in erect impassiveness, trying the bolts and the window-catches, and went away again, having said never a word. I had planned to ask her if I might

now have a bed to myself, but somehow my
courage failed me, so stern and majestic was her
aspect.

I took the desired boon without asking, and
dreamed of her as a darkling and relentless Joab
in petticoats, slaying her own son Jeff as he hung
by his hay-coloured hair in one of the apple-trees
of our orchard.

## IV

On all the other farms roundabout, this mid-
August was a slack season. The hired men and
boys did a little early fruit-picking, a little
berrying, a little stone-drawing, but for the most
part they could be seen idling about the woods or
along the river down toward Juno Mills, with gun
or fish-pole. Only upon the one farm whose turn
it was that week to be visited by the itinerant
threshing-machine, was any special activity visible.

It was well known, however, that we were not
to get the threshing-machine at all. How it was
managed, I never understood. Perhaps the other
farmers combined in some way to overawe or
persuade the owners of the machine into refusing
it to Abner Beech. More likely he scented the
chance of a refusal, and was too proud to put
himself in its way by asking. At all events, we
three—Abner, Hurley, and I—had to manage

the threshing ourselves, on the matched-wood floor of the carriage barn. All the fishing I did that year was in the prolific but unsubstantial waters of dreamland.

I did not work much, it is true, with the flail, but I lived all day in an atmosphere choked with dust and chaff, my ears deafened with the ceaseless whack! whack! of the hard-wood clubs, bringing on fresh shocks of grain, and acting as general helper.

By toiling late and early we got this task out of the way just when the corn was ready to cut. This great job taxed the energies of the two men, the one cutting, the other stacking, as they went. My own share of the labour was to dig the potatoes and pick the eating-apples—a quite portentous enough undertaking for a lad of twelve. All this kept me very much to myself. There was no chance to talk during the day, and at night I was glad to drag my tired limbs off to bed before the girls had fairly cleared the supper things away. A weekly newspaper—*The World* —came regularly to the post-office at the Corners for us, but we were so overworked that often it lay there for weeks at a time, and even when some one went after it, nobody but Abner cared to read it.

So far as I know, no word ever came from Jeff. His name was never mentioned among us.

It was now past the middle of September. Except for the fall ploughing on fields that were to be put to grass under the grain in the spring— which would come much later—the getting in of the root crops, and the husking, our season's labours were pretty well behind us. The women folk had toiled like slaves as well, taking almost all the chores about the cattle-barns off our shoulders, and carrying on the butter-making without bothering us. Now that a good many cows were drying up, it was their turn to take things easy, too. But the girls, instead of being glad at this, began to borrow unhappiness over the certainty that there would be no husking-bees on the Beech farm.

One heard no other subject discussed now, as we sat of a night in the kitchen. Even when we foregathered in the living-room instead, the Babcock and the Underwood girl talked in ostentatiously low tones of the hardship of missing such opportunities for getting beaux, and having fun. They recalled to each other, with tones of longing, this and that husking-bee of other years—now one held of a moonlight night in the field itself, where the young men pulled the stacks down and dragged them to where the girls sat in a ring on big pumpkins, and merriment, songs, and chorused laughter chased the happy hours along ; now of a bee held in the late

wintry weather, where the men went off to the
barn by themselves, and husked till they were
tired, and then, with warning whoops, came back
to where the girls were waiting for them in the
warm, hospitable farmhouse, and the frolic began,
with cider and apples and pumpkin-pies, and old
Lem Hornbeck's fiddle to lead the dancing.

Alas! they shook their empty heads and
mourned, there would be no more of those
delightful times! Nothing definite was ever said
as to the reason for our ostracism from the sports
and social enjoyments of the season. There was
no need for that. We all knew too well that it
was Abner Beech's politics which made us outcasts, but even these two complaining girls did
not venture to say so in his hearing. Their talk,
however, grew at last so persistently querulous
that " M'rye " bluntly told them one night to
" shut up about husking-bees," following them out
into the kitchen for that purpose, and speaking
with unaccustomed acerbity. Thereafter we heard
no more of their grumbling, but in a week or two
" Till " Babcock left for her home over on the
Dutch Road, and began circulating the report
that we prayed every night for the success of Jeff
Davis.

It was on a day in the latter half of September,
perhaps the 20th or 21st—as nearly as I am able
to make out from the records now—that Hurley

and I started off with a double team and our big box-waggon, just after breakfast, on a long day's journey. We were taking a heavy load of potatoes in to market at Octavius, twelve miles distant ; thence we were to drive out an additional three miles to a cooper-shop, and bring back as many butter-firkins as we could stack up behind us, not to mention a lot of groceries of which " M'rye " gave me a list.

It was a warm, sweet-aired, hazy autumn day, with a dusky red sun sauntering idly about in the sky, too indolent to cast more than the dimmest and most casual suggestion of a shadow for anything or anybody. The Irishman sat, round-backed and contented, on the very high seat overhanging the horses, his elbows on his knees, and a little black pipe turned upside down in his mouth. He would suck satisfiedly at this for hours after the fire had gone out, until, my patience exhausted, I begged him to light it again. He seemed almost never to put any new tobacco into this pipe, and to this day it remains a twin-mystery to me why its contents neither burned themselves to nothing nor fell out.

We talked a good deal, in a desultory fashion, as the team plodded their slow way into Octavius. Hurley told me, in answer to the questions of a curious boy, many interesting and remarkable things about the old country, as he always called it, and

more particularly about his native part of it,
which was on the sea-shore within sight of Skib-
bereen. He professed always to be filled with
longing to go back, but at the same time guarded
his tiny personal expenditure with the greatest
solicitude, in order to save money to help one of
his relations to get away. Once, when I taxed
him with this inconsistency, he explained that life
in Ireland was the most delicious thing on earth,
but you had to get off at a distance of some
thousands of miles to really appreciate it.

Naturally there was considerable talk between
us, as well, about Abner Beech and his troubles.
I don't know where I could have heard it, but
when Hurley first came to us I at once took it for
granted that the fact of his nationality made him
a sympathiser with the views of our household.
Perhaps I only jumped at this conclusion from
the general ground that the few Irish who in those
days found their way into the farm-country were
held rather at arm's-length by the community,
and must in the nature of things feel drawn to
other outcasts. At all events, I made no mistake.
Hurley could not have well been more vehemently
embittered against abolitionism and the war than
Abner was, but he expressed his feelings with
much greater vivacity and fluency of speech. It
was surprising to see how much he knew about
the politics and political institutions of a strange

country, and how excited he grew about them when any one would listen to him. But as he was a small man, getting on in years, he did not dare air these views down at the Corners. The result was that he and Abner were driven to commune together, and mutually inflamed each other's passionate prejudices—which was not at all needful.

When at last, shortly before noon, we drove into Octavius, I jumped off to fill one portion of the grocery errands, leaving Hurley to drive on with the potatoes. We were to meet at the little village tavern for dinner.

He was feeding the horses in the hotel shed when I rejoined him an hour or so later. I came in, bursting with the importance of the news I had picked up—scattered, incomplete, and even incoherent news, but of the most exciting sort. The awful battle of Antietam had happened two or three days before, and nobody in all Octavius was talking or thinking of anything else. Both the Dearborn County regiments had been in the thick of the fight, and I could see from afar, as I stood on the outskirts of the throng in front of the post-office, some long strips of paper posted up beside the door, which men said contained a list of our local dead and wounded. It was hopeless, however, to attempt to get anywhere near this list, and nobody, whom I questioned,

knew anything about the names of those young
men who had marched away from our Four
Corners. Some one did call out, though, that the
telegraph had broken down, or gone wrong, and
that not half the news had come in as yet. But
they were all so deeply stirred up, so fiercely
pushing and hauling to get toward the door, that
I could learn little else.

This was what I began to tell Hurley, with
eager volubility, as soon as I got in under the
shed. He went on with his back to me, impassively measuring out the oats from the bag,
and clearing aside the stale hay in the manger,
the impatient horses rubbing at his shoulders
with their noses the while. Then, as I was nearly
done, he turned and came out to me, slapping
the fodder mess off his hands.

He had a big fresh cut running transversely
across his nose and cheek, and there were stains
of blood in the grey stubble of beard on his chin.
I saw too that his clothes looked as if he had
been rolled on the dusty road outside.

"Sure, then, I'm after hearin' the news myself,"
was all he said.

He drew out from beneath the waggon seat a
bag of crackers and a hunk of cheese, and, seating
himself on an overturned barrel, began to eat.
By a gesture I was invited to share this meal, and
did so, sitting beside him. Something had hap-

pened, apparently, to prevent our having dinner in the tavern.

I fairly yearned to ask him what this something was, and what was the matter with his face, but it did not seem quite the right thing to do, and presently he began mumbling, as much to himself as to me, a long and broken discourse, from which I picked out that he had mingled with a group of lusty young farmers in the market-place, asking for the latest intelligence, and that while they were conversing in a wholly amiable manner, one of them had suddenly knocked him down and kicked him, and that thereafter they had pursued him with curses and loud threats half-way to the tavern. This and much more he proclaimed between mouthfuls, speaking with great rapidity and in so much more marked a brogue than usual, that I understood only a fraction of what he said.

He professed entire innocence of offence in the affair, and either could not or would not tell what it was he had said to invite the blow. I daresay he did in truth richly provoke the violence he encountered, but at the time I regarded him as a martyr, and swelled with indignation every time I looked at his nose.

I remained angry, indeed, long after he himself had altogether recovered his equanimity and whimsical good spirits. He waited outside on

the seat, while I went in to pay for the baiting of
the horses, and it was as well that he did, I fancy,
because there were half a dozen brawny farm-
hands and villagers standing about the bar, who
were laughing in a stormy way over the episode
of the " Copperhead Paddy " in the market.

We drove away, however, without incident of
any sort—sagaciously turning off the main street
before we reached the post-office block, where the
congregated crowd seemed larger than ever. There
seemed to be some fresh tidings, for several scattering outbursts of cheering reached our ears after
we could no longer see the throng ; but, so far
from stopping to inquire what it was, Hurley put
whip to the horses, and we rattled smartly along
out of the excited village into the tranquil, scythe-
shorn country.

The cooper to whom we now went for our
butter-firkins was a long-nosed, lean, and taciturn
man, whom I think of always as with his apron
tucked up at the corner, and his spectacles on his
forehead, close under the edge of his square
brow-paper cap. He had had word that we were
coming, and the firkins were ready for us. He
helped us load them in dead silence, and with a
gloomy air.

Hurley desired the sound of his own voice.
" Well, then, sir," he said, as our task neared
completion, " 'tis worth coming out of our way

these fifteen miles to lay eyes on such fine, grand firkins as these same—such an elegant shape on 'em, an' put together wid such nateness!"

"You could git 'em just as good at Hagadorn's," said the cooper, curtly, "within a mile of your place."

"Huh!" cried Hurley, with contempt, "Haggydorn is it? Faith, we'll not touch him or his firkins ayether! Why, man, they're not fit to mention the same day wid yours. Ah, just look at the darlins, will ye, that nate an' clane a Christian could ate from 'em!"

The cooper was blarney-proof. "Hagadorn's are every smitch as good!" he repeated, ungraciously.

The Irishman looked at him perplexedly, then shook his head as if the problem were too much for him, and slowly clambered up to the seat. He had gathered up the lines, and we were ready to start, before any suitable words came to his tongue.

"Well, then, sir," he said, "anything to be agreeable. If I hear a man speaking a good word for your firkins, I'll dispute him."

"The firkins are well enough," growled the cooper at us, "an' they're made to sell, but I ain't so almighty tickled about takin' Copperhead money for 'em that I want to clap my wings an crow over it."

He turned scornfully on his heel at this, and
we drove away. The new revelation of our friend-
lessness depressed me, but Hurley did not seem to
mind it at all. After a philosophic comparative
remark about the manners of pigs run wild in a
bog, he dismissed the affair from his thoughts
altogether, and hummed cheerful words to melancholy tunes half the way home, what time he was
not talking to the horses or tossing stray conversational fragments at me.

My own mind soon enough surrendered itself
to harrowing speculations about the battle we
had heard of. The war had been going on now
for over a year, but most of the fighting had
been away off in Missouri and Tennessee, or
on the lower Mississippi, and the reports had not
possessed for me any keen direct interest. The
idea of men from our own district—young men
whom I had seen, perhaps fooled with, in the
hayfield only ten weeks before—being in an
actual storm of shot and shell, produced a faint-
ness at the pit of my stomach. Both Dearborn
County regiments were in it, the crowd said.
Then of course our men must have been there—
our hired men, and the Philips boys, and Byron
Truax, and his cousin Alonzo, and our Jeff ! And
if so many others had been killed, why not they
as well ?

" Antietam " still has a power to arrest my

eyes on the printed page, and disturb my ears in the hearing, possessed by no other battle name. It seems now as if the very word itself had a terrible meaning of its own to me, when I first heard it that September afternoon—as if I recognised it to be the label of some awful novelty, before I knew anything else. It had its fascination for Hurley, too, for presently I heard him crooning to himself, to one of his queer old Irish tunes, some doggerel lines which he had made up to rhyme with it—three lines with "cheat 'em,' ' beat 'em," and "Antietam," and then his pet refrain, "Says the Shan van Vocht."

This levity jarred unpleasantly upon the mood into which I had worked myself, and I turned to speak of it, but the sight of his bruised nose and cheek restrained me. He had suffered too much for the faith that was in him to be lightly questioned now. So I returned to my grisly thoughts, which now all at once resolved themselves into a conviction that Jeff had been killed outright. My fancy darted to meet this notion, and straightway pictured for me a fantastic battle-field by moonlight, such as was depicted in Lossing's books, with overturned cannon-wheels and dead horses in the foreground, and in the centre, conspicuous above all else, the inanimate form of Jeff Beech, with its face coldly radiant in the moonshine.

" I guess I'll hop off and walk a spell," I said, under the sudden impulse of this distressing visitation.

It was only when I was on the ground, trudging along by the side of the waggon, that I knew why I had got down. We were within a few rods of the Corners, where one road turned off to go to the post-office. " Perhaps it'd be a good idea for me to find out if they've heard anything more—I mean —anything about Jeff," I suggested. " I'll just look in and see, and then I can cut home cross lots."

The Irishman nodded and drove on.

I hung behind, at the Corners, till the waggon had begun the ascent of the hill, and the looming bulk of the firkins made it impossible that Hurley could see which way I went. Then, without hesitation, I turned instead down the other road which led to " Jee " Hagadorn's.

## V

TIME was when I had known the Hagadorn house, from the outside at least, as well as any other in the whole township. But I had avoided that road so long now, that when I came up to the place it seemed quite strange to my eyes.

For one thing, the flower garden was much

bigger than it had formerly been. To state it differently, Miss Esther's marigolds and columbines, hollyhocks and peonies, had been allowed to usurp a lot of space where sweet-corn, potatoes and other table-truck used to be raised. This not only greatly altered the aspect of the place, but it lowered my idea of the practical good sense of its owners.

What was more striking still, was the general air of decrepitude and decay about the house itself. An eaves-trough had fallen down ; half the cellar door was off its hinges, standing up against the wall ; the chimney was ragged and broken at the top ; the clap-boards had never been painted, and now were almost black with weather-stain and dry rot. It positively appeared to me as if the house was tipping sideways, over against the little cooper-shop adjoining it—but perhaps that was a trick of the waning evening light. I said to myself that if we were not prospering on the Beech farm, at least our foe " Jee " Hagadorn did not seem to be doing much better himself.

In truth, Hagadorn had always been among the poorest members of our community, though this by no means involves what people in citie think of as poverty. He had a little place of nearly two acres, and then he had his coopering business ; with the two he ought to have got on comfortably enough. But a certain contrariness in his nature seemed to be continually interfering with this.

This strain of conscientious perversity ran through all we knew of his life before he came to us, just as it had dominated the remainder of his career. He had been a well-to-do man some ten years before, in a city in the western part of the State, with a big cooper-shop, and a lot of men under him, making the barrels for a large brewery. (It was in these days, I fancy, that Esther took on that urban polish which the younger Benaiah missed.) Then he got the notion in his head that it was wrong to make barrels for beer, and threw the whole thing up. He moved into our neighbourhood with only money enough to buy the old Andrews place, and build a little shop.

It was a good opening for a cooper, and Hagadorn might have flourished if he had been able to mind his own business. The very first thing he did was to offend a number of our biggest butter-makers by taxing them with sinfulness in also raising hops, which went to make beer. For a long time they would buy no firkins of him. Then, too, he made an unpleasant impression at church. As has been said, our meeting-house was a union affair, that is to say, no one denomination being numerous enough to have an edifice of its own, all the farmers round about—Methodists, Baptists, Presbyterians, and so on—joined in paying the expenses. The travelling preachers who came to us represented these great sects, with lots of minute shadings off into Hard-shell, Soft-shell, Free-will, and other subdivided mysteries which I never understood. Hagadorn had a denomination all to himself, as might have been expected from the man. What the name of it was I seem never to have heard ; perhaps it had no name at all. People used to say, though, that he behaved like a Shouting Methodist.

This was another way of saying that he made a nuisance of himself in church. At prayer-meetings, in the slack seasons of the year, he would pray so long, and with such tremendous shouting and fury of gestures, that he had regularly to be asked to stop, so that those who had taken the trouble to learn and practise new hymns might have a chance to be heard. And then he would out-sing all the others, not knowing the tune in the least, and cause added confusion by yelling out shrill " Amens ! " between the bars. At one time quite a number of the leading people ceased attending church at all, on account of his conduct.

He added heavily to his theological unpopularity, too, by his action in another matter. There was a wealthy and important farmer living over on the west side of Agrippa Hill, who was a Universalist. The expenses of our union meet-

ing-house were felt to be a good deal of a burden,
and our elders, conferring together, decided that
it would be a good thing to waive ordinary prejudices, and let the Universalists come in, and have
their share of the preaching. It would be more
neighbourly, they felt, and they would get a sub-
scription from the Agrippa Hill farmer. He
assented to the project, and came over four or five
Sundays with his family and hired help, listened
unflinchingly to orthodox sermons full of sulphur
and blue flames, and put money on the plate
every time. Then a Universalist preacher occupied the pulpit one Sunday, and preached a highly
inoffensive and non-committal sermon, and " Jee "
Hagadorn stood up in his pew and violently
denounced him as an infidel, before he had
descended the pulpit steps. This created a painful scandal. The Universalist farmer, of course
never darkened that church door again. Some
of our young men went so far as to discuss the
ducking of the obnoxious cooper in the horse-
pond. But he himself was neither frightened
nor ashamed.

At the beginning, too, I suppose that his taking
up Abolitionism made him enemies. Dearborn
County gave Franklin Pierce a big majority in
'52, and the bulk of our farmers, I know, were in
that majority. But I have already dwelt upon
the way in which all this changed in the years

just before the War.   Naturally enough, Hagadorn's
position also changed.   The rejected stone became
the head of the corner.   The tiresome fanatic of
the 'fifties was the inspired prophet of the 'sixties.
People still shrank from giving him undue credit
for their conversion, but they felt themselves swept
along under his influence none the less.

But just as his unpopularity kept him poor in
the old days, it seemed that now the reversed condition was making him still poorer.   The truth
was, he was too excited to pay any attention to
his business.   He went off to Octavius three or
four days a week to hear the news, and when he
remained at home, he spent much more time
standing out in the road discussing politics and
the conduct of the war with passers-by, than he did
over his staves and hoops.   No wonder his place
was run down.

The house was dark and silent, but there was
some sort of a light in the cooper-shop beyond.
My hope had been to see Esther rather than her
wild old father, but there was nothing for it but to
go over to the shop.   I pushed the loosely fitting
door back on its leathern hinges, and stepped over
the threshold.   The resinous scent of newly-cut
wood and the rustle of the shavings under my feet
had the effect, somehow, of filling me with timidity.
It required an effort to not turn and go out again.

The darkened and crowded interior of the tiny

work-place smelt as well, I noted now, of smoke. On the floor before me was crouched a shapeless figure—bending in front of the little furnace, made of a section of stove-pipe, which the cooper used to dry the insides of newly-fashioned barrels. A fire in this—half-blaze, half-smudge—gave forth the light I had seen from without, and the smoke which was making my nostrils tingle. Then I had to sneeze, and the kneeling figure sprang on the instant from the floor.

It was Esther who stood before me, coughing a little from the smoke, and peering inquiringly at me. " Oh—is that you, Jimmy ? " she asked, after a moment of puzzled inspection in the dark.

She went on, before I had time to speak, in a nervous, half-laughing way : " I've been trying to roast an ear of corn here, but it's the worst kind of a failure. I've watched ' Ni ' do it a hundred times, but with me it always comes out half-scorched and half-smoked. I guess the corn is too old now, any way. At all events, its tougher than Pharaoh's heart."

She held out to me, in proof of her words, a blackened and unseemly roasting-ear. I took it, and turned it slowly over, looking at it with the grave scrutiny of an expert. Several torn and opened sections showed where she had been testing it with her teeth. In obedience to her " See if you don't think it's too old," I took a diffident bite, at a respectful distance from the marks of her experiments. It was the worst I had ever tasted.

"I came over to see if you'd heard anything—any news," I said, desiring to get away from the corn subject.

"You mean about Tom?" she asked, moving so that she might see me more plainly.

I had stupidly forgotten about that transformation of names. "Our Jeff, I mean," I made answer.

"His name is Thomas Jefferson. *We* call him Tom," she explained; "that other name is too horrid. Did—did his people tell you to come and ask *me?*"

I shook my head. "Oh no!" I replied with emphasis, implying by my tone, I daresay, that they would have had themselves cut up into sausage-meat first.

The girl walked past me to the door, and out to the road-side, looking down toward the bridge with a lingering, anxious gaze. Then she came back, slowly.

"No, we have no news!" she said, with an effort at calmness. "He wasn't an officer, that's why. All we know is that the brigade his regiment is in lost 141 killed, 560 wounded, and 38 missing. That's all!" She stood in the doorway, her hands clasped tight, pressed against her bosom. "*That's all!*" she repeated, with a choking voice.

Suddenly she started forward, almost ran across the few yards of floor, and, throwing herself down in the darkest corner, where only dimly one could see an old buffalo-robe spread over a heap of staves, began sobbing as if her heart must break.

Her dress had brushed over the stove-pipe, and scattered some of the embers beyond the sheet of tin it stood on. I stamped these out, and carried the other remnants of the fire out doors. Then I returned, and stood about in the smoky little shop, quite helplessly listening to the moans and convulsive sobs which rose from the obscure corner. A bit of a candle in a bottle stood on the shelf by the window. I lighted this, but it hardly seemed to improve the situation. I could see her now, as well as hear her—huddled face downward upon the skin, her whole form shaking with the violence of her grief. I had never been so unhappy before in my life.

At last—it may not have been very long, but it seemed hours—there rose the sound of voices outside on the road. A waggon had stopped, and some words were being exchanged. One of the voices grew louder—came nearer ; the other died off, ceased altogether, and the waggon could be heard driving away. On the instant the door was pushed sharply open, and " Jee " Hagadorn

stood on the threshold, surveying the interior of
his cooper-shop with gleaming eyes.

He looked at me ; he looked at his daughter
lying in the corner ; he looked at the charred
mess on the floor—yet seemed to see nothing of
what he looked at. His face glowed with a
strange excitement—which in another man I
should have set down to drink.

" Glory be to God ! Praise to the Most High !
Mine eyes have seen the glory of the coming of
the Lord ! " he called out, stretching forth his
hands in a rapturous sort of gesture I remembered
from class-meeting days.

Esther had leaped to her feet with squirrel-like
swiftness at the sound of his voice, and now stood
before him, her hands nervously clutching at each
other, her reddened, tear-stained face a-fire with
eagerness.

" Has word come—is he safe ?—have you
heard ? " so her excited questions tumbled over
one another, as she grasped " Jee's " sleeve and
shook it in feverish impatience.

" The day has come ! The year of Jubilee is
here ! " he cried, brushing her hand aside, and
staring with a fixed, ecstatic, open-mouthed smile
straight ahead of him. " The words of the
Prophet are fulfilled ! "

" But Tom !—*Tom !* " replied the girl, piteously.
' The list has come ? You know he is safe ? "

" Tom ! *Tom !* " old " Jee " repeated after her, but with an emphasis contemptuous, not solicitous. " Perish a hundred Toms—yea—ten thousand ! for one such day as this ! 'For the Scarlet Woman of Babylon is overthrown, and bound with chains and cast into the lake of fire. Therefore, in one day shall her plagues come, death, and mourning, and famine ; and she shall be utterly burned with fire ; for strong is the Lord God which judged her ! ' "

He declaimed these words in a shrill, high-pitched voice, his face upturned, and his eyes half-closed. Esther plucked despairingly at his sleeve once more. " But have you seen ?—is *his* name ?—you must have seen ? " she moaned, incoherently.

" Jee " descended for the moment from his plane of exaltation. " I *didn't* see ! " he said, almost peevishly. " Lincoln has signed a proclamation freeing all the slaves ! What do you suppose I care for your Toms and Dicks and Harrys, on such a day as this ? 'Woe ! woe ! the great city Babylon, the strong city ! For in one hour is thy judgment come ! ' "

The girl tottered back to her corner, and threw herself limply down upon the buffalo-robe again, hiding her face in her hands.

I pushed my way past the cooper, and trudged cross-lots home in the dark, tired, disturbed, and very hungry, but thinking most of all that if I had been worth my salt, I would have hit "Jee" Hagadorn with the adze that stood up against the door-still.

## VI

It must have been a fortnight before we learned that Jeff Beech and Byron Truax had both been reported missing. I say "we," but I do not know when Abner Beech came to hear about it. One of the hired girls had seen the farmer get up from his chair, with the newly arrived weekly *World* in his hand, walk over to where his wife sat, and direct her attention to a line of the print with his finger. Then, still in silence, he had gone over to the bookcase, opened the drawer where he kept his account-books, and locked the journal up therein.

We took it for granted that thus the elderly couple had learned the news about their son. They said so little nowadays, either to each other or to us, that we were driven to speculate upon their dumb-show, and find meanings for ourselves in their glances and actions. No one of us could imagine himself or herself venturing to mention Jeff's name in their hearing.

Down at the Corners, though, and all about our district, people talked of very little else.

Antietam had given a bloody welcome to our
little group of warriors. Ray Watkins and Lon
Truax had been killed outright; and Ed Philips
was in the hospital, with the chances thought to
be against him. Warner Pitts, our other hired
man, had been wounded in the arm, but not
seriously, and thereafter behaved with such conspicuous valour that it was said he was to be pro-
moted from being a sergeant to a lieutenancy.
All these things, however, paled in interest after
the first few days before the fascinating mystery
of what had become of Jeff and Byron. The
loungers about the grocery-store evenings took
sides as to the definition of " missing." Some
said it meant being taken prisoners ; but it was
known that at Antietam the Rebels made next to
no captives. Others held that " missing " soldiers
were those who had been shot, and who crawled
off somewhere in the woods out of sight to die.
A lumber-man from Juno Mills, who was up on
a horse-trade, went so far as to broach still a third
theory, viz., that " missing " soldiers were those
who had run away under fire, and were ashamed
to show their faces again. But this malicious
suggestion could not, of course, be seriously con-
sidered.

Meanwhile, what little remained of the fall
farm work went on as if nothing had happened.
The root crops were dug, the fodder got in, and

E

the late apples gathered.    Abner had a cider mill
of his own, but we sold a much larger share of our
winter apples than usual.    Less manure was drawn
out on to the fields than in other autumns, and it
looked as if there was to be little or no fall
ploughing.    Abner went about his tasks in a heavy,
spiritless way these days, doggedly enough, but
with none of his old-time vim.    He no longer had
pleasure even in abusing Lincoln and the war
with Hurley.    Not Antietam itself could have
broken his nerve, but at least it silenced his
tongue.

Warner Pitts came home on a furlough, with a
fine new uniform, shoulder-straps, and sword, and
his arm in a sling.    I say "home," but the only
roof he had ever slept under in these parts was
ours, and now he stayed as a guest at Squire
Avery's house, and never came near our farm.    He
was a tall, brown-faced, sinewy fellow, with curly
hair and a pushing manner.    Although he had
been only a hired man he now cut a great dash
down at the Corners, with his shoulder-straps and
his officer's cape.    It was said that he had declined several invitations to husking-bees, and that
when he left the service, at the end of his time, he
had a place ready for him in some city as a clerk
in a dry goods store—that is, of course, if he did
not get to be colonel or general.    From time to
time he was seen walking out through the dry,

rustling leaves with Squire Avery's oldest
daughter.

This important military genius did not seem
able, however, to throw much light upon the where-
abouts of the two "missing" boys. From what I
myself heard him say about the battle, and from
what others reported of his talk, it seems that in
the very early morning Hooker's line—a part of
which consisted of Dearborn County men—moved
forward through a big cornfield, the stalks of which
were much higher than the soldiers' heads. When
they came out, the rebels opened such a hideous
fire of cannon and musketry upon them from the
woods close by, that those who did not fall
were glad to run back again into the corn for
shelter. Thus all became confusion, and the men
were so mixed up that there was no getting them
together again. Some went one way, some another,
through the tall corn rows, and Warner Pitts could
not remember having seen either Jeff or Byron at
all after the march began. Parts of the regiment
formed again out on the road toward the Dunker
church, but other parts found themselves half a
mile away among the fragments of a Michigan
regiment, and a good many more were left lying
in the fatal cornfield. Our boys had not been
traced among the dead, but that did not prove
that they were alive. And so we were no wiser
than before.

Warner Pitts only nodded in a distant way to me when he saw me first, with a cool " Hello, youngster ! " I expected that he would ask after the folks at the farm which had been so long his home, but he turned to talk with some one else, and said never a word. Once, some days after-ward, he called out as I passed him, " How's the old Copperhead ? " and the Avery girl who was with him laughed aloud, but I went on without answering. He was already down in my black-books, in company with pretty nearly every other human being round about.

The list of enemies was indeed so full that there were times when I felt like crying over my isolation. It may be guessed, then, how rejoiced I was one afternoon to see Ni Hagadorn squeeze his way through our orchard-bars, and saunter across under the trees to where I was at work sorting a heap of apples into barrels. I could have run to meet him, so grateful was the sight of any friendly, boyish face. The thought that perhaps after all he had not come to see me in particular, and that possibly he brought some news about Jeff, only flashed across my mind after I had smiled a broad welcome upon him, and he stood leaning against a barrel munching the biggest russet he had been able to pick out.

" Abner to home ? " he asked, after a pause of

neighbourly silence. He hadn't come to see me after all.

" He's around the barns somewhere," I replied ; adding, upon reflection, "have you heard something fresh ? "

Ni shook his sorrel head, and buried his teeth deep into the apple. " No, nothin'," he said, at last, with his mouth full, " only thought I'd come up an' talk it over with Abner."

The calm audacity of the proposition took my breath away. " He'll boot you off from the place if you try it," I warned him.

But Ni did not scare easily. " Oh, no," he said, with light confidence, " me and Abner's all right."

As if to put this assurance to the test, the figure of the farmer was at this moment visible, coming toward us down the orchard road. He was in his shirt-sleeves, with the limp, discoloured old broad-brimmed felt hat he always wore pulled down over his eyes. Though he no longer held his head so proudly erect as I could remember it, there were still suggestions of great force and mastership in his broad shoulders and big beard, and in the solid, long-gaited manner of his walk. He carried a pitchfork in his hand.

"Hello, Abner ! " said Ni, as the farmer came up and halted, surveying each of us in turn with an impressive scrutiny.

" How 'r' ye ! " returned Abner, with cold
civility. I fancied he must be surprised to see
the son of his enemy here, calmly gnawing his
way through one of our apples, and acting as if
the place belonged to him. But he gave no signs
of astonishment, and after some words of direction
to me concerning my work, started to move on
again toward the barns.

Ni was not disposed to be thus cheated out of
his conversation : " Seen Warner Pitts since he's
got back ? " he called out, and at this the farmer
stopped and turned round. " You'd hardly know
him now," the butcher's assistant went on, with
cheerful briskness. " Why you'd think he'd never
hoofed it over ploughed land in all his life. He's
got his boots blacked up every day, and his hair
greased, and a whole new suit of broadcloth, with
shoulder-straps and brass buttons, and a sword—
he brings it down to the Corners every evening,
so that the boys at the store can heft it—and
he's——"

" What do I care about all this ? " broke in
Abner. His voice was heavy, with a growling
ground-note, and his eyes threw out an angry
light under the shading hat-brim. " He can go to
the devil, and take his sword with him, for all o'
me ! "

Hostile as was his tone, the farmer did not
again turn on his heel. Instead, he seemed to

suspect that Ni had something more important to say, and looked him steadfastly in the face.

" That's what I say, too," replied Ni, lightly. " What's beat me is how such a fellow as that got to be an officer right from the word ' go ! '—and him the poorest shote in the whole lot. Now if it had a' been Spencer Phillips I could understand it—or Bi Truax, or—or your Jeff—"

The farmer raised his fork menacingly, with a wrathful gesture. " Shet up ! " he shouted ; " shet up, I say ! or I'll make ye ! "

To my great amazement Ni was not at all affected by this demonstration. He leaned smilingly against the barrel, and picked out another apple—a spitzenberg this time.

" Now look-a here, Abner," he said, argumentatively, " what's the good o' gittin' mad ? When I've had my say out, why, if you don't like it you needn't, an' nobody's a cent the wuss off. Of course, if you come down to hard-pan, it ain't none o' my business——"

" No," interjected Abner, in grim assent, " it ain't none o' your business ! "

" But there is such a thing as being neighbourly," Ni went on, undismayed, " an' meaning things kindly, and taking 'em as they're meant."

" Yes, I know them kindly neighbours of mine ! " broke in the farmer with acrid irony ; " I've summered 'em and I've wintered 'em, and the

Lord deliver me from the whole caboodle of 'em !
A meaner lot of cusses never cumbered this foot-
stool ! "

" It takes all sorts o' people to make up a
world," commented this freckled and sandy headed
young philosopher, testing the crimson skin of
his apple with a tentative thumb-nail.    " Now you
ain't got anything in particular agin me, have
you ? "

" Nothin' except your breed," the farmer
admitted.    The frown with which he had been
regarding Ni had softened just the least bit in
the world.

" That don't count," said Ni, with easy confidence.    " Why, what does breed amount to,
anyway ?   You ought to be the last man alive
to lug that in—you, who've up an' soured on
your own breed—your own son Jeff ! "

I looked to see Abner lift his fork again, and
perhaps go even further in his rage.    Strangely
enough, there crept into his sunburnt, massive
face, at the corners of the eyes and mouth, something like the beginnings of a puzzled smile.
" You're a cheeky little cuss, anyway ! " was his
final comment.    Then his expression hardened
again.    " Who put you up to coming here, and
talking like this to me ? " he demanded, sternly.

" Nobody—hope to die ! " protested Ni.    " It's
all my own spec.    It riled me to see you moping

round up here all alone by yourself, not knowing what'd become of Jeff, an' making believe to yourself you didn't care, and so givin' yourself away to the whole neighbourhood."

"Damn the neighbourhood!" said Abner, fervently.

"Well, they talk about the same of you," Ni proceeded, with an air of impartial candour. "But all that don't do you no good, and don't do Jeff no good!"

"He made his own bed, and he must lay on it," said the farmer, with dogged firmness.

"I ain't saying he mustn't," remonstrated the other. "What I'm gittin' at is that you'd feel easier in your mind if you knew where that bed was—and so'd M'rye!"

Abner lifted his head. "His mother feels jest as I do," he said. "He sneaked off behind our backs to jine Lincoln's nigger-worshippers, an' levy war on fellow-countrymen of his'n who'd done him no harm, an' whatever happens to him it serves him right. I ain't much of a hand to lug in Scripter to back up my argyments—like some folks you know of—but my feeling is: 'Whoso taketh up the sword shall perish by the sword!' And so says his mother too!"

"Hm-m!" grunted Ni, with ostentatious incredulity. He bit into his apple, and there ensued a momentary silence. Then, as soon as he was able to speak, this astonishing boy said : " Guess I'll have a talk with M'rye about that herself."

The farmer's patience was running emptings. " No ! " he said, severely, " I forbid ye ! Don't ye dare say a word to her about it. She don't want to listen to ye ; an' I don't know what's possessed *me* to stand round and gab about my private affairs with you like this, either. I don't bear ye no ill-will. If fathers can't help the kind of sons they bring up, why, still less can ye blame sons on account of their fathers. But it ain't a thing I want to talk about any more, either now or any other time. That's all."

Abner put the fork over his shoulder, as a sign that he was going, and that the interview was at an end. But the persistent Ni had a last word to offer, and he left his barrel and walked over to the farmer.

" See here," he said, in more urgent tones than he had used before. " I'm goin' South, an' I'm going to find Jeff if it takes a leg ! I don't know how much it'll cost. I've got a little of my own saved up, an' I thought p'r'aps--p'r'aps you'd like to———"

After a moment's thought the farmer shook his head. " No," he said, gravely, almost reluctantly. " It's agin my principles. You know me—Ni— you know I've never been a near man, let alone a mean man. An' you know, too, that if Je—if that boy had behaved half-way decent, there ain't anything under the sun I wouldn't 'a' done for him. But this thing—I'm obleeged to ye for offrin', but—No! it's agin my principles. Still, I'm obleeged to ye. Fill your pockets with them spitzenbergs, if they taste good to ye."

With this, Abner Beech turned and walked resolutely off.

Left alone with me, Ni threw away the half-eaten apple he had held in his hand. "I don't want any of his dummed old spitzenbergs," he said, pushing his foot into the heap of fruit on the ground, in a meditative way.

"Then you ain't a-going South?" I queried.

"Yes I am," he replied, with decision. "I can work my way somehow. Only don't you whisper a word about it to any living soul, d'ye mind!"

Two or three days after that we heard that Ni Hagadorn had left for unknown parts. Some said he had gone to enlist—it seems that, despite his youth and small stature in my eyes, he would have been acceptable to the enlistment standards of the day—but the major opinion was that much dime-novel reading had inspired him with the notion of becoming a trapper in the mystic Far West.

I alone possessed the secret of his disappearance—unless, indeed, his sister knew—and no

one will ever guess what struggles I had to keep
from confiding it to Hurley.

## VII

SOON the fine weather was at an end. One day
it was soft and warm, with a tender blue haze
over the distant woods and a sun like a blood-
orange in the tranquil sky, and birds twittering
about among the elders and sumac along the
rail fences. And the next day everything was
grey and lifeless and desolate, with fierce winds
sweeping over the bare fields, and driving the
cold rain in sheets before them.

Some people—among them Hurley—said it
was the equinoctial that was upon us. Abner
Beech ridiculed this, and proved by the dictionary
that the equinoctial meant September 22nd,
whereas it was now well-nigh the end of October.
The Irishman conceded that in books this might
be so, but stuck wilfully to it that in practice the
equinoctial came just before winter set in. After
so long a period of saddened silence brooding
over our household, it was quite a relief to hear
the men argue this question of the weather.

Down at the Corners old farmers had wrangled
over the identity of the equinoctial ever since I
could remember. It was pretty generally agreed

that each year along some time during the fall, there came a storm which was properly entitled to that name, but at this point harmony ended. Some insisted that it came before Indian Summer, some that it followed that season, and this was further complicated by the fact that no one was ever quite sure when it *was* Indian Summer. There were all sorts of rules for recognising this delectable time of year, rules connected, I recall, with the opening of chestnut burrs, the movement of birds, and various other incidents in Nature's great processional, but these rules rarely came right in our rough latitude, and sometimes never came at all—at least did not bring with them anything remotely resembling Indian Summer, but made our autumn one prolonged and miserable succession of storms. And then it was an especially trying trick to pick out the equinoctial from the lot—and even harder still to prove to sceptical neighbours that you were right.

Whatever this particular storm may have been, it came too soon. Being so short-handed on the farm, we were much behind in the matter of drawing our produce to market. And now, after the first day or two of rain, the roads were things to shudder at. It was not so bad getting to and from the Corners, for Agrippa Hill has a gravel formation, but beyond the Corners, whichever way one went over the bottom lands of the Nedahma

Valley, it was a matter of lashing the panting
teams through seas of mud punctuated by abysmal
pitch-holes, into which the •wheels slumped over
their hubs, and quite generally stuck till they were
pried out with fence-rails.

Abner Beech was exceptionally tender in his
treatment of live-stock. The only occasion I
ever heard of on which he was tempted into using
his big fists upon a fellow-creature, was once,
long before my time, when one of his hired-men
struck a refractory cow over its haunches with a
shovel. He knocked this man clean through the
stanchions. Often Jeff and I used to feel that he
carried his solicitude for horseflesh too far—particularly when we wanted to drive down to the
creek for a summer evening swim, and he thought
the teams were too tired.

So now he would not let us hitch up and drive
into Octavius with even the lightest loads, on
account of the horses. It would be better to
wait, he said, until there was sledding ; then we
could slip in in no time. He pretended that all
the signs this year pointed to an early winter.

The result was that we were more than ever
shut off from news of the outer world. The
weekly paper which came to us was full, I remember, of political arguments and speeches—for
a Congress and Governor were to be elected a
few weeks hence—but there were next to no

tidings from the front. The war, in fact, seemed to have almost stopped altogether, and this paper spoke of it as a confessed failure. Farmer Beech and Hurley, of course, took the same view, and their remarks quite prepared me from day to day to hear that peace had been concluded.

But down at the Corners a strikingly different spirit reigned. It quite surprised me, I know, when I went down on occasion for odds and ends of groceries which the bad roads prevented us from getting in town, to discover that the talk there was all in favour of having a great deal more war than ever.

This store at the Corners was also the post-office, and, more important still, it served as a general rallying-place for the men-folks of the neighbourhood after supper. Lee Watkins, who kept it, would rather have missed a meal of victuals any day than not to have had the " boys " come in of an evening, and sit or lounge around discussing the situation. Many of them were very old boys now, garrulous seniors who re-membered " Matty " Van Buren, as they called him, and told weird stories of the Anti-Masonry days. These had the well-worn armchairs nearest the stove, in cold weather, and spat tobacco-juice on its hottest parts with a precision born of long-time experience. The younger fellows accommodated themselves about the outer circle, squatting on boxes, or with one leg over a barrel, sampling the sugar and crackers and raisins in an absent-minded way each evening, till Mrs. Watkins came out and put the covers on. She was a stout, peevish woman in bloomers, and they said that her husband, Lee, couldn't have run the post-office for twenty-four hours if it hadn't been for her. We understood that she was a Woman's Rights' woman, which some held was much the same as believing in Free Love. What was certain, however, was that she did not believe in free lunches out of her husband's barrels and cases.

The chief flaw in this village parliament was the absence of an opposition. Among all the accustomed assemblage of men who sat about, their hats well back on their heads, their mouths full of strong language and tobacco, there was none to disagree upon any essential feature of the situation with the others. To secure even the merest semblance of variety, those whose instincts were cross-grained had to go out of their way to pick up trifling points of difference, and the arguments over these had to be spun out with the greatest possible care, to be kept going at all. I should fancy, however, that this apparent concord only served to keep before their minds, with added persistency, the fact that there *was* an opposition, nursing its heretical wrath in solitude

up on the Beech farm. At all events, I seemed
never to go into the grocery of a night without
hearing bitter remarks, or even curses, levelled at
our household.

It was from these casual visits—standing about
on the outskirts of the gathering, beyond the
feeble ring of light thrown out by the kerosene
lamp on the counter—that I learned how deeply
the Corners were opposed to peace. It appeared
from the talk here that there was something very
like treason at the front. The victory at Antietam
—so dearly bought with the blood of our own
people—had been, they said, of worse than no
use at all. The defeated Rebels had been allowed
to take their own time in crossing the Potomac
comfortably. They had not been pursued or
molested since, and the Corners could only account for this on the theory of treachery at Union
headquarters. Some only hinted guardedly at
this. Others declared openly that the North was
being sold out by its own generals. As for old
"Jee" Hagadorn, who came in almost every night,
and monopolised the talking all the while he was
present, he made no bones of denouncing Mc-
Clellan and Porter as traitors who must be
hanged.

He comes before me as I write—his thin form
quivering with excitement, the red stubbly hair
standing up all round his drawn and livid face,

his knuckles rapping out one fierce point after
another on the candle-box, as he filled the hot
little room with angry declamation. "Go it
Jee!" "Give 'em Hell!" "Hanging's too good
for 'em!" his auditors used to exclaim in encouragement, whenever he paused for breath, and then
he would start off again still more furiously, till
he had to gasp after every word, and screamed,
"Lincoln-ah!" "Richmond-ah!" "Antietam-
ah!" and so on, into our perturbed ears. Then I
would go home, recalling how he had formerly
shouted about "Adam-ah!" and "Eve-ah!" in
church, and marvelling that he had never worked
himself into a fit, or broken a blood-vessel.

So between what Abner and Hurley said on the
farm, and what was proclaimed at the Corners, it
was pretty hard to figure out whether the war
was going to stop, or go on much worse than
ever.

Things were still in this doubtful state when
election Tuesday came round. I had not known
or thought about it, until, at the breakfast-table
Abner said that he guessed he and Hurley would
go down and vote before dinner. He had some
days before secured a package of ballots from the
organisation of his party at Octavius, and these he
now took from one of the bookcase drawers, and
divided between himself and Hurley.

"They won't be much use, I dessay, peddling

'em at the polls," he said, with a grim momentary smile, " but, by the Eternal, we'll vote 'em ! "

" As many of 'em as they'll be allowin' us,' added Hurley, in chuckling qualification.

They were very pretty tickets in those days, with marbled and plaided backs in brilliant colours, and spreading eagles in front, over the printed captions. In other years I had shared with the urchins of the neighbourhood the excitement of scrambling for a share of these ballots, after they had been counted, and tossed out of the boxes. The conditions did not seem to be favourable for a repetition of that this year, and apparently this occurred to Abner, for of his own accord he handed me over some dozen of the little packets, each tied with a thread, and labelled, " State," " Congressional," " Judiciary," and the like. He, moreover, consented—the morning chores being out of the way—that I should accompany them to the Corners. The ground had frozen stiff overnight, and the road lay in hard uncompromising ridges between the tracks of yesterday's wheels. The two men swung along down the hill ahead of me, with resolute strides and their heads proudly thrown back, as if they had been going into battle. I shuffled on behind in my new boots, also much excited. The day was cold and raw.

The polls were fixed up in a little building

next to the post-office—a one-story frame struct-
ure where Lee Watkins kept his bob-sleigh and
oil-barrels, as a rule. These had been cleared out
into the yard, and a table and some chairs put in
in their place. A pane of glass had been taken out
of the window. Through this aperture the voters,
each in his turn, passed their ballots, to be placed
by the inspectors in the several boxes ranged
along the window-sill inside. A dozen or more
men, mainly in army overcoats, stood about on the
side-walk or in the road outside, stamping their
feet for warmth, and slapping their shoulders with
their hands, between the fingers of which they
held little packets of tickets like mine—that is to
say, they were like mine in form and brilliancy of
colour, but I knew well enough that there the
resemblance ended abruptly. A yard or so from
the window two posts had been driven into the
ground, with a board nailed across to prevent undue crowding.

Abner and Hurley marched up to the polls
without a word to any one, or any sign of recog-
nition from the bystanders. Their appearance,
however, visibly awakened the interest of the
Corners, and several young fellows who were
standing on the grocery steps sauntered over in
their wake to see what was going on. These,
with the ticket-pedlers, crowded up close to the
window now, behind our two men.

"Abner Beech!" called the farmer through the open pane, in a defiant voice. Standing on tiptoe, I could just see the heads of some men inside, apparently looking through the registry books. No questions were asked, and in a minute or so Abner had voted and stood aside a little, to make room for his companion.

"Timothy Joseph Hurley!" shouted our hired man, standing on his toes to make himself taller, and squaring his weazened shoulders.

"Got your naturalization papers?" came out a sharp, gruff inquiry through the window-sash.

"That I have!" said the Irishman, wagging his head in satisfaction at having foreseen this trick, and winking blandly into the wall of stolid, hostile faces encircling him. "That I have!"

He drew forth an old and crumpled envelope from his breast-pocket, and extracted some papers from its ragged folds which he passed through to the inspector. The latter just cast his eye over the documents and handed them back.

"Them ain't no good!" he said, curtly.

"What's that you're saying?" cried the Irishman. "Sure I've voted on thim same papers every year since 1856, an' niver a man gainsaid me. No good, is it? Huh!"

"Why ain't they no good?" boomed in Abner Beech's deep, angry voice. He had moved back to the window.

" Because they ain't, that's enough ! " returned the inspector. " Don't block up the window, there !   Others want to vote ! "

" I'll have the law on yez ! " shouted Hurley. " I'll swear me vote in !   I'll—I'll——"

" Aw, shut up, you Mick ! " some one called out close by, and then there rose another voice farther back in the group : " Don't let him vote !   One Copperhead's enough in Agrippa ! "

" I'll have the law——" I heard Hurley begin again, at the top of his voice, and Abner roared out something I could not catch.   Then, as in a flash, the whole cluster of men became one confused whirling tangle of arms and legs, sprawling and wrestling on the ground, and from it rising the repellent sound of blows upon flesh, and a discordant chorus of grunts and curses.   Big chunks of icy mud flew through the air, kicked up by the boots of the men as they struggled.   I saw the two posts with the board weave under the strain, then give way, some of the embattled group tumbling over them as they fell.   It was wholly impossible to guess who was who in this writhing and tossing mass of fighters.   I danced up and down in a frenzy of excitement, watching this wild spectacle, and, so I was told years afterwards, screaming with all my might and main.

Then all at once there was a mighty upheaval, and a big man half-scrambled, half-hurled himself

to his feet. It was Abner, who had wrenched
one of the posts bodily from under the others, and
swung it now high in air. Some one clutched it,
and for the moment stayed its descent, yelling,
meanwhile, " Look out ! Look out ! " as though
life itself depended on the volume of his voice.

The ground cleared itself as if by magic. On
the instant there was only Abner standing there
with the post in his hands, and little Hurley
beside him, the lower part of his face covered
with blood, and his coat torn half from his back.
The others had drawn off, and formed a semi-
circle just out of reach of the stake, like farm-dogs
round a wounded bear at bay. Two or three of
them had blood about their heads and necks.

There were cries of " Kill him ! " and it was
said afterward that Roselle Upman drew a pistol,
but if he did others dissuaded him from using it.
Abner stood with his back to the building, breathing hard, and a good deal covered with mud, but
eyeing the crowd with a masterful ferocity, and
from time to time shifting his hands to get a new
grip on that tremendous weapon of his. He said
not a word.

The Irishman, after a moment's hesitation,
wiped some of the blood from his mouth and jaw,
and turned to the window again. " Timothy
Joseph Hurley ! " he shouted in, defiantly.

This time another inspector came to the front

—the owner of the tanyard over on the Dutch road, and a man of importance in the district. Evidently there had been a discussion inside.

" We will take your vote if you want to swear it in," he said, in a pacific tone, and though there were some dissenting cries from the crowd without, he read the oath, and Hurley mumbled it after him.

Then, with some difficulty, he sorted out from his pocket some torn and mud-stained packets of tickets, picked the cleanest out from each, and voted them—all with a fine air of unconcern.

Abner Beech marched out behind him now with a resolute clutch on the stake. The crowd made reluctant way for them, not without a good many truculent remarks, but with no offer of actual violence. Some of the more boisterous ones, led by Roselle Upman, were for following them, and renewing the encounter beyond the Corners. But this, too, came to nothing, and when I at last ventured to cross the road and join Abner and Hurley, even the cries of " Copperhead !" had died away.

The sun had come out, and the frosty ruts had softened to stickiness. The men's heavy boots picked up whole sections of plastic earth as they walked in the middle of the road up the hill.

" What's the matter with your mouth ? " asked

Abner at last, casting a sidelong glance at his companion. " It's been a-bleeding."

Hurley passed an investigating hand carefully over the lower part of his face, looked at his reddened fingers, and laughed aloud.

" I'd a fine grand bite at the ear of one of them," he said, in explanation. " 'Tis no blood o' mine."

Abner knitted his brows. " That ain't the way we fight in this country," he said, in tones of displeasure. " Biting men's ears ain't no civilised way of behaving."

" 'Twas not much of a day for civilisation," remarked Hurley, lightly ; and there was no further conversation on our homeward tramp.


## VIII

THE election had been on Tuesday, November 4th. Our paper, containing the news of the result, was to be expected at the Corners on Friday morning. But long before that date we had learned—I think it was Hurley who found it out —that the Abolitionists had actually been beaten in our Congressional district. It was so amazing a thing that Abner could scarcely credit it, but it was apparently beyond dispute. For that matter, one hardly needed further evidence than the dejected way in which Philo Andrews and Myron Pierce and other followers of " Jee " Hagadorn hung their heads as they drove past our place.

Of course it had all been done by the vote in the big town of Tecumseh, away at the other end of the district, and by those towns surrounding it where the Mohawk Dutch were still very numerous. But this did not at all lessen the exhilaration with which the discovery that the Radicals of our own Dearborn County had been snowed under, filled our breasts. Was it not wonderful to think of, that these heroes of remote Adams and Jay Counties should have been at work redeeming the district on the very day when the two votes of our farm marked the almost despairing low-water mark of the cause in Agrippa !

Abner could hardly keep his feet down on the ground or floor when he walked, so powerfully did the tidings of this achievement fill his veins. He said the springs of his knees kept jerking upward, so that he wanted to kick and dance all the while. Janey Wilcox, who, though a meek and silent girl, was a wildly bitter partisan, was all eagerness to light a bonfire out on the knoll in front of the house on Thursday night, so that every mother's son of them down at the Corners might see it, but Abner thought it would be better to wait until we had the printed facts before us.

I could hardly wait to finish breakfast Friday morning, so great was my zeal to be off to the post-office. It was indeed not altogether daylight when I started at quick-step down the hill. Yet, early as I was, there were some twenty people inside Lee Watkins's store when I arrived, all standing clustered about the high square row of glass-faced pigeon-holes reared on the farther end of the counter, behind which could be seen Lee and his sour-faced wife sorting over the mail by lamp-light. " Jee " Hagadorn was in this group and Squire Avery, and most of the other prominent citizens of the neighbourhood. All were deeply restless.

Every minute or two some one of them would shout : " Come, Lee, give us out *one* of the papers, anyway ! " But for some reason Mrs. Watkins was inexorable. Her pursed-up lips and resolute expression told us plainly that none would be served till all were sorted. So the impatient waiters bided their time under protest, exchanging splenetic remarks under their breath. We must have stood there three-quarters of an hour.

At last Mrs. Watkins wiped her hands on the apron over her bloomers. Everybody knew the signal, and on the instant a dozen arms were stretched vehemently toward Lee, struggling for precedence. In another moment wrappers had been ripped off and sheets flung open. Then the store was alive with excited voices. " Yes, sir !

It's true ! The Copperheads have won ! " " *Tribune*
concedes Seymour's election ! " " We're beaten in
the district by less'n a hundred ! " " Good-bye,
human liberty ! " " Now we know how Lazarus
felt when he was licked by the dogs ! " and so on—
a stormy warfare of wrathful ejaculations.

In my turn I crowded up, and held out my hand
for the paper I saw in the box. Lee Watkins
recognised me, and took the paper out to deliver
to me. But at the same moment his wife, who
had been hastily scanning the columns of some
other journal, looked up and also saw who I was.
With a lightning gesture she threw out her hand,
snatched our *World* from her husband's grasp,
and threw it spitefully under the counter.

" There ain't nothing for *you !* " she snapped at
me. " Pesky Copperhead rag ! " she muttered to
herself.

Although I had plainly seen the familiar wrapper,
and understood her action well enough, it never
occurred to me to argue the question with Mrs.
Watkins. Her bustling, determined demeanour,
perhaps also her bloomers, had always filled me
with awe. I hung about for a time, avoiding her
range of vision, until she went out into her kitchen.
Then I spoke with resolution to Lee :

" If you don't give me that paper," I said, " I'll
tell Abner, an' he'll make you sweat for it."

The postmaster stole a cautious glance kitchen-ward. Then he made a swift, diving movement under the counter, and furtively thrust the paper out at me.

"Scoot!" he said, briefly, and I obeyed him.

Abner was simply wild with bewildered delight over what this paper had to tell him. Even my narrative about Mrs. Watkins, which ordinarily would have thrown him into transports of rage, provoked only a passing sniff. "They've only got two more years to hold that post-office," was his only remark upon it.

Hurley and Janey Wilcox and even the Underwood girl came in, and listened to Abner reading out the news. He shirked nothing, but waded manfully through long tables of figures and meaningless catalogues of counties in other States, the names of which he scarcely knew how to pronounce: "'Five hundred and thirty-one townships in Wisconsin give Brown 21,409, Smith 16,329, Ferguson 802, a Republican loss of 26.' Do you see that, Hurley? It's everywhere the same." "'Kalapoosas County elects Republican Sheriff for first time in history of party.' That isn't so good, but it's only one out of ten thousand." "'Four hundred and six townships in Massachusetts show a net Democratic loss of—' pshaw! there ain't nothing in that! Wait till the other towns are heard from."

So Abner read on and on, slapping his thigh with his free hand whenever anything specially good turned up. And there was a great deal that we felt to be good. The State had been carried. Besides our Congressman, many others had been elected in unlooked-for places—so much so that the paper held out the hope that Congress itself might be ours. Of course Abner at once talked as if it were already ours. Resting between paragraphs, he told Hurley and the others that this settled it. The war must now surely be abandoned, and the seceding States invited to return to the Union on terms honourable to both sides.

Hurley had assented with acquiescent nods to everything else. He seemed to have a reservation on this last point. "An' what if they won't come?" he asked.

"Let 'em stay out, then," replied Abner, dogmatically. "This war—this wicked war between brothers—must stop. That's the meaning of Tuesday's votes. What did you and I go down to the Corners and cast our ballots for?—why, for peace!"

"Well, somebody else got my share of it, then," remarked Hurley, with a rueful chuckle.

Abner was too intent upon his theme to notice. "Yes, peace!" he repeated, in the deep vibrating tones of his class-meeting manner. "Why, just

think what's been a-goin' on! Great armies
raised, hundreds of thousands of honest men
taken from their work and set to murdering each
other, whole deestricks of country torn up by
the roots, homes desolated, the land filled with
widows and orphans, and every house a house of
mourning."

Mrs. Beech had been sitting, with her mending
basket on her knee, listening to her husband, like
the rest of us. She shot to her feet now as these
last words of his quivered in the air, paying no
heed to the basket or its scattered contents on
the floor, but putting her apron to her eyes, and
making her way thus past us, half-blindly, into
her bedroom. I thought I heard the sound of a
sob as she closed the door.

That the stately, proud, self-contained mistress
of our household should act like this before us all
was even more surprising than Seymour's election. We stared at one another in silent
astonishment.

" M'rye ain't feelin' over 'n' above well," Abner
said at last, apologetically. " You girls ought to
spare her all you kin."

One could see, however, that he was as puzzled
as the rest of us. He rose to his feet, walked
over to the stove, rubbed his boot meditatively
against the hearth for a minute or two, then came
back again to the table. It was with a visible

effort that he finally shook off this mood, and
forced a smile to his lips.

"Well, Janey," he said, with an effort at briskness, "you kin go ahead with your bonfire now.
I guess I've got some old barrels for ye over in
the cowbarn."

But, having said this, he turned abruptly and
followed his wife into the little chamber off the
living-room.


## IX


THE next day, Saturday, was my birthday. I
celebrated it by a heavy cold, with a bursting
headache and chills chasing each other down my
back. I went out to the cow-barn with the two
men before daylight, as usual, but felt so bad
that I had to come back to the house before
milking was half over. The moment M'rye saw
me, I was ordered on to the sick-list.

The Beech homestead was a good place to be
sick in. Both M'rye and Janey had a talent in
the way of fixing up tasty little dishes for invalids,
and otherwise ministering to their comfort, which
year after year went a-begging, simply because all
the men-folk kept so well. Therefore, when the
rare opportunity did arrive, they made the most
of it. I had my feet and legs put into a bucket

of hot water, and wrapped round with burdock
leaves. Janey prepared for my breakfast some
soft toast—not the insipid and common milk-
toast — but each golden-brown slice treated
separately on a plate, first moistened with scalding
water, then peppered, salted, and buttered, with a
little cold milk on top of all. I ate this sump-
tuous breakfast at my leisure, ensconced in
M'rye's big cushioned rocking-chair, with my feet
and legs, well tucked up in a blanket-shawl,
stretched out on another chair, comfortably near
the stove.

It was taken for granted that I had caught my
cold out around the bonfire the previous evening—
and this conviction threw a sort of patriotic
glamour about my illness, at least in my own
mind.

The bonfire had been a famous success.
Though there was a trifle of rain in the air, the
barrels and mossy discarded old fence-rails burned
like pitch-pine, and when Hurley and I threw on
armfuls of brush, the sparks burst up with a roar
into .a flaming column which we felt must be
visible all over our side of Dearborn County. At
all events, there was no doubt about its being
seen and understood down at the Corners, for
presently our enemies there started an answering
bonfire, which glowed from time to time with
such a peculiarly concentrated radiance that

Abner said Lee Watkins must have given them
some of his kerosene-oil barrels. The thought of
such a sacrifice as this on the part of the postmaster rather disturbed Abner's mind, raising, as
it did, the hideous suggestion that possibly later
returns might have altered the election results.
But when Hurley and I dragged forward and
tipped over into the blaze the whole side of an
old abandoned corn-crib, and heaped dry brush on
top of that, till the very sky seemed afire above
us, and the stubble-fields down the hill-side were
all ruddy in the light, Abner confessed himself
reassured. Our enthusiasm was so great that it
was nearly ten o'clock before we went to bed,
having first put the embers out, lest a rising wind
during the night should scatter sparks and work
mischief.

I had all these splendid things to think of next
day, along with my headache and the shivering
spine, and they tipped the balance toward satisfaction. Shortly after breakfast, M'rye made a
flaxseed poultice and muffled it flabbily about my
neck, and brought me also some boneset-tea to
drink. There was a debate in the air as between
castor-oil and senna, fragments of which were
borne in to me when the kitchen-door was open.
The Underwood girl alarmed me by steadily
insisting that her sister-in-law always broke up
sick-headaches with a mustard-plaster put raw on

the back of the neck. Every once in a while one
of them would come in and address to me the
stereotyped formula ; " Feel any better ? " and I
as invariably answered, "No." In reality, though,
I was lazily comfortable all the time, with
Lossing's " Field Book of the War of 1812,"
lying open on my lap, to look at when I felt
inclined. This book was not nearly so interesting
as the one about the Revolution, but a grandfather of mine had marched as a soldier up to
Sackett's Harbour in the later war, though he did
not seem to have had any fighting to do after he
got there, and in my serious moods I always felt
it my duty to read about his war instead of the
other.

So the day passed along, and dusk began to
gather in the living-room. The men were off
out-doors somewhere, and the girls were churning
in the butter-room. M'rye had come in with her
mending, and sat on the opposite side of the
stove, at intervals casting glances over its flat top
to satisfy herself that my poultice had not sagged
down from its proper place, and that I was in
other respects doing as well as could be expected.

Conversation between us was hardly to be
thought of, even if I had not been so drowsily
indolent. M'rye was not a talker, and preferred
always to sit in silence, listening to others, or,
better still, going on at her work with no sounds

at all to disturb her thoughts.    These long periods
of meditation, and the sedate gaze of her black,
penetrating eyes, gave me the feeling that she
must be much wiser than other women, who could
not keep still at all, but gabbled everything the
moment it came into their heads.

We had sat thus for a long, long time, until I
began to wonder how she could sew in the waning
light, when all at once, without lifting her eyes
from her work, she spoke to me.

" D' you know where Ni Hagadorn's gone to?'
she asked me, in a measured, impressive voice.

" He—he—told me he was a-goin' away," I
made answer, with weak evasiveness.

" But where ? Down South ? "    She looked up,
as I hesitated, and flashed that darkling glance
of hers at me.    " Out with it ! " she commanded.
" Tell me the truth ! "

Thus adjured, I promptly admitted that Ni had
said he was going South, and could work his way
somehow.    " He's gone, you know," I added, after
a pause, " to try and find—that is, to hunt around
after——"

" Yes, I know," said M'rye, sententiously, and
another long silence ensued.

She rose after a time, and went out into the
kitchen, returning with the lighted lamp.    She
set this on the table, putting the shade down on
one side so that the light should not hurt my

eyes, and resumed her mending. The yellow glow
thus falling upon her gave to her dark, severe,
high-featured face a duskier effect than ever. It
occurred to me that Molly Brant, that mysteriously
fascinating and bloody Mohawk queen who left
such an awful reddened mark upon the history of
her native Valley, must have been like our M'rye.
My mind began sleepily to clothe the farmer's
wife in blankets and chains of wampum, with
eagles' feathers in her raven hair, and then to drift
vaguely off over the threshold of Indian dreamland, when suddenly, with a start, I became conscious that some unexpected person had entered
the room by the veranda door behind me.

The rush of cold air from without had awakened
me and told me of the entrance. A glance at
M'rye's face revealed the rest. She was staring
at the newcomer with a dumbfounded expression
of countenance, her mouth half-open with sheer
surprise. Still staring, she rose and tilted the
lamp-shade in yet another direction, so that the
light was thrown upon the stranger. At this I
turned in my chair to look.

It was Esther Hagadorn who had come in !

There was a moment's awkward silence, and
then the school-teacher began hurriedly to speak.
" I saw you were alone from the veranda—I was
so nervous, it never occurred to me to rap—the
curtains being up—I—I walked straight in."

As if in comment upon this statement, M'rye marched across the room, and pulled down both curtains over the veranda windows. With her hand still upon the cord of the second shade, she turned and again dumbly surveyed her visitor.

Esther flushed visibly at this reception, and had to choke down the first words that came to her lips. Then she went on better : " I hope you'll excuse my rudeness. I really did forget to rap. I came upon very special business. Is Ab——Mr. Beech at home ? "

"Won't you sit down ? " said M'rye, with a glum effort at civility. " I expect him in presently."

The school-ma'am, displaying some diffidence, seated herself in the nearest chair, and gazed at the wall-paper with intentness. She had never seemed to notice me at all—indeed had spoken of seeing M'rye alone through the window—and I now coughed, and stirred to readjust my poultice, but she did not look my way. M'rye had gone back to her chair by the stove, and taken up her mending again.

" You'd better lay off your things. You won't feel 'em when you go out," she remarked, after an embarrassing period of silence, investing the formal phrases with chilling intention.

Esther made a fumbling motion at the loop of her big mink cape, but did not unfasten it.

" I—I don't know *what* you think of me," she began, at last, and then nervously halted.

" Mebbe it's just as well you don't," said M'rye, significantly, darning away with long sweeps of her arm, and bending attentively over her stocking and ball.

"I can understand your feeling hard," Esther went on, still eyeing the sprawling blue figures on the wall, and plucking with her fingers at the furry tails on her cape. "And—I *am* to blame, *some*, I can see now—but it didn't seem so, *then*, to either of us."

" It ain't no affair of mine," remarked M'rye, when the pause came, " but if that's your business with Abner, you won't make much by waiting. Of course it's nothing to me, one way or t' other."

Not another word was exchanged for a long time. From where I sat I could see the girl's lips tremble, as she looked steadfastly into the wall. I felt certain that M'rye was darning the same place over and over again, so furiously did she keep her needle flying.

All at once she looked up angrily. " Well," she said, in loud, bitter tones : " why not out with what you've come to say, 'n' be done with it ? You've heard something, *I* know ! "

Esther shook her head. " No, Mrs. Beech," she said, with a piteous quaver in her voice, " I— I haven't heard anything ! "

The sound of her own broken utterances seemed to affect her deeply. Her eyes filled with tears, and she hastily got out a handkerchief from her muff, and began drying them. She could not keep from sobbing aloud a little.

M'rye deliberately took another stocking from the heap in the basket, fitted it over the ball, and began a fresh task—all without a glance at the weeping girl.

Thus the two women still sat, when Janey came in to lay the table for supper. She lifted the lamp off to spread the cloth, and put it on again ; she brought in plates and knives and spoons, and arranged them in their accustomed places—all the while furtively regarding Miss Hagadorn with an incredulous surprise. When she had quite finished she went over to her mistress, and, bending low, whispered so that we could all hear quite distinctly : " Is *she* goin' to stay to supper ? "

M'rye hesitated, but Esther lifted her head and put down the handkerchief instantly. " Oh, no ! " she said, eagerly : " don't think of it ! I must hurry home as soon as I've seen Mr. Beech." Janey went out with an obvious air of relief.

Presently there was a sound of heavy boots out in the kitchen being thrown on to the floor, and then Abner came in. He halted in the doorway, his massive form seeming to completely fill it, and devoted a moment or so to taking in the novel spectacle of a neighbour under his roof. Then he advanced, walking obliquely till he could see distinctly the face of the visitor. It stands to reason that he must have been surprised, but he gave no sign of it.

"How d'do, Miss," he said, with grave politeness, coming up and offering her his big hand.

Esther rose abruptly, peony-red with pleasurable confusion, and took the hand stretched out to her. "How d'do, Mr. Beech," she responded with eagerness, "I—I came up to see you—a— about something that's very pressing."

"It's blowing up quite a gale outside," the farmer remarked, evidently to gain time the while he scanned her face in a solemn, thoughtful way, noting, I doubt not, the swollen eyelids and stains of tears, and trying to guess her errand. "Shouldn't wonder if we had a foot o' snow before morning."

The school-teacher stood in doubt how best to begin what she had to say, so that Abner had time, after he lifted his inquiring gaze from her, to run a master's eye over the table.

"Have Janey lay another place!" he said, with authoritative brevity.

As M'rye rose to obey, Esther broke forth : "Oh, no, please don't! Thank you so much,

Mr. Beech—but really I can't stop—truly, I mustn't think of it."

The farmer merely nodded a confirmation of his order to M'rye, who hastened out to the kitchen.

" It'll be there for ye, anyway," he said. " Now sit down again, please."

It was all as if he was the one who had the news to tell, so naturally did he take command of the situation. The girl seated herself, and the farmer drew up his armchair and planted himself before her, keeping his stockinged feet under the rungs for politeness' sake.

" Now, Miss," he began, just making it civilly plain that he preferred not to utter her hated paternal name, " I don't know no more'n a babe unborn what's brought you here. I'm sure, from what I know of ye, that you wouldn't come to this house jest for the sake of coming, or to argy things that can't be, an' mustn't be, argied. In one sense, we ain't friends of yours here, and there's a heap o' things that you and me don't want to talk about, because they'd only lead to bad feelin', and so we'll leave 'em all severely alone. But in another way, I've always had a liking for you. You're a smart girl, and a scholar into the bargain, and there ain't so many o' that sort knocking around in these parts that a man like myself, who's fond of books an' learnin', wants to be unfriendly to them there is. So now you can figure out pretty well where the chalk line lays, and we'll walk on it."

Esther nodded her head. "Yes, I understand," she remarked, and seemed not to dislike what Abner had said.

"That being so, what is it?" the farmer asked, with his hands on his knees.

"Well, Mr. Beech," the school-teacher began, noting with a swift side glance that M'rye had returned, and was herself rearranging the table. "I don't think you can have heard it, but some important news has come in during the day. There seem to be different stories, but the gist of them is that a number of the leading Union generals have been discovered to be traitors, and McClellan has been dismissed from his place at the head of the army, and ordered to return to his home in New Jersey under arrest, and they say others are to be treated in the same way, and Fath—*some* people think it will be a hanging matter, and——"

Abner waived all this aside with a motion of his hand. "It don't amount to a hill o' beans," he said, placidly. "It's jest spite, because we licked 'em at the elections. Don't you worry your head about *that*."

Esther was not reassured. "That isn't all," she went on, nervously. "They say there's been discovered a big conspiracy, with secret sympathizers all over the North."

"Pooh!" commented Abner. "We've heer'n tell o' that before."

"All over the North," she continued, "with the intention of bringing across infected clothes from Canada, and spreading the small-pox among us, and——"

The farmer laughed outright; a laugh embittered by contempt. "What cock-'n'-bull story'll be hatched next!" he said. "You don't mean to say you—a girl with a head on her shoulders like *you*—give ear to such tomfoolery as that! Come now, honest Injin, do you mean to tell me *you* believed all this?"

"It don't so much matter, Mr. Beech," the girl replied, raising her face to his, and speaking more confidently ; "it don't matter at all what I believe. I'm talking of what they believe down at the Corners."

"The Corners be jiggered!" exclaimed Abner, politely, but with emphasis.

Esther rose from the chair. "Mr. Beech," she declared, impressively, "they're coming up here to-night. That bonfire of yours made 'em mad. It's no matter how I learned it—it wasn't from father—I don't know that he knows anything about it, but they're coming *here!* and—and Heaven only knows what they're going to do when they get here."

The farmer rose also, his huge figure towering above that of the girl, as he looked down at her over his beard. He no longer dissembled his stockinged feet. After a moment's pause he said : " So that's what you came to tell me, eh ? "

The school-ma'am nodded her head. " I couldn't bear not to," she explained, simply.

" Well, I'm obleeged to ye," Abner remarked, with gravity. " Whatever comes of it, I'm obleeged to ye."

He turned at this, and walked slowly out into the kitchen, leaving the door open behind him. " Pull on your boots again," we heard him say, presumably to Hurley. In a minute or two he returned, with his own boots on, and bearing over his arm the old double-barrelled shot-gun which always hung above the kitchen mantelpiece. In his hands he had two shot-flasks, the little tobacco-bag full of buckshot, and a powder-horn. He laid these on the open shelf of the bookcase, and, after fitting fresh caps on the nipples put the gun beside them.

" I'd be all the more sot on your stayin' to supper," he remarked, looking again at Esther, " only if there *should* be any unpleasantness, why, I'd hate like sin to have you mixed up in it. You see how I'm placed."

Esther did not hesitate a moment. She walked over to where M'rye stood by the table replenishing the butter-plate. "I'd be very glad indeed to stay, Mr. Beech," she said, with winning frankness, "if I may."

"There's the place laid for you," commented M'rye, impassively. Then, catching her husband's eye, she added the perfunctory assurance, "You're entirely welcome."

Hurley and the girls came in now, and all except me took their seats about the table. Both Abner and the Irishman had their coats on, out of compliment to company. M'rye brought over a thick slice of fresh-buttered bread with brown sugar on it, and a cup of weak tea, and put them beside me on a chair. Then the evening meal went forward, the farmer talking in a fragmentary way about the crops and the weather. Save for an occasional response from our visitor, the rest maintained silence. The Underwood girl could not keep her fearful eyes from the gun lying on the bookcase, and protested that she had no appetite, but Hurley ate vigorously, and had a smile on his wrinkled and swarthy little face.

The wind outside whistled shrilly at the windows, rattling the shutters, and trying its force in explosive blasts which seemed to rock the house on its stone foundations. Once or twice it shook the veranda-door with such violence that the folk at the table instinctively lifted their heads, thinking some one was there.

Then, all at once, above the confusion of the storm's noises, we heard a voice rise, high and clear, crying:

"*Smoke the damned Copperhead out!*"

## X

"THAT was Roselle Upman that hollered," remarked Janey Wilcox, breaking the agitated silence which had fallen upon the supper-table. "You can tell it's him because he's had all his front teeth pulled out."

"I wasn't born in the woods to be skeert by an owl!" replied Abner, with a great show of tranquillity, helping himself to another slice of bread. "Miss, you ain't half making out a supper!"

But this bravado could not maintain itself. In another minute there came a loud chorus of angry yells, heightened at its finish by two or three pistol shots. Then Abner pushed back his chair and rose slowly to his feet, and the rest sprang up all around the table.

"Hurley," said the farmer, speaking as deliberately as he knew how, doubtless with the idea of reassuring the others, "you go out into the kitchen with the women folks, an' bar the woodshed door, an' bring in the axe with you to stan' guard over

the kitchen door.  I'll look out for this part o'
the house myself."

"I want to stay in here with you, Abner," said
M'rye.

"No, you go out with the others!" commanded the master with firmness, and so they
all filed out, with no hint whatever of me.  The
shadow of the lamp-shade had cut me off
altogether from their thoughts.

Perhaps it is not surprising that my recollections of what now ensued should lack definiteness
and sequence.  The truth is, that my terror at
my own predicament, sitting there with no covering for my feet and calves but the burdock leaves
and that absurd shawl, swamped everything else
in my mind.  Still, I do remember some of it.

Abner strode across to the bookcase and took
up the gun, his big thumb resting determinedly
on the hammers.  Then he marched to the door,
threw it wide open, and planted himself on the
threshold, looking out into the darkness.

"What's your business here, whoever you are?"
he called out, in deep defiant tones.

"We've come to take you and Paddy out for a
little ride on a rail!" answered the same shrill
mocking voice we heard at first.  Then others
took up the chorus.  "We've got some pitch a'
heating round in the back yard!"  "You won't
catch cold; there's plenty o' feathers!  "Tell the

Irishman here's some more ears for him to chaw on!" "Come out an' take your Copperhead medicine!"

There were yet other cries which the howling wind tore up into inarticulate fragments, and then a scattering volley of cheers, again emphasised by pistol shots. While the crack of these still chilled my blood, a more than usually violent gust swooped round Abner's burly figure, and blew out the lamp.

Terrifying as the first instant of utter darkness was, the second was recognizable as a relief. I at once threw myself out of the chair, and crept along back of the stove to where my stockings and boots had been put to dry. These I hastened, with much trembling awkwardness, to pull on, taking pains to keep the big square old stove between me and that open veranda door.

"Guess we won't take no ride to-night!" I heard Abner roar out, after the shouting had for the moment died away.

"You got to have one!" came back the original voice. "It's needful for your complaint!"

"I've got somethin' here that'll fit *your* complaint!" bellowed the farmer, raising his gun. "Take warnin'—the first cuss that sets foot on this stoop, I'll bore a four-inch hole clean through him. I've got squirrel shot, an' I've got buckshot, an' there's plenty more behind—so take your choice!"

There were a good many derisive answering yells and hoots, and some one again fired a pistol in the air, but nobody offered to come up on the veranda.

Emboldened by this, I stole across the room now to one of the windows, and lifting a corner of the shade, strove to look out. At first there was nothing whatever to be seen in the utter blackness. Then I made out some faint reddish sort of diffused light in the upper air, which barely sufficed to indicate the presence of some score or more dark figures out in the direction of the pump. Evidently they *had* built a fire around in the back yard, as they said—probably starting it there so that its light might not disclose their identity.

This looked as if they really meant to tar-and-feather Abner and Hurley. The expression was familiar enough to my ears, and, from pictures in stray illustrated weeklies that found their way to the Corners, I had gathered some general notion of the procedure involved. The victim was stripped, I knew, and daubed over with hot melted pitch; then a pillow-case of feathers was emptied over him, and he was forced astride a fence-rail, which the rabble hoisted on their shoulders and ran about with. But my fancy balked at and refused the task of imagining Abner Beech in this humiliating posture. At least it was clear to my mind that a good many fierce and bloody things would happen first.

Apparently this had become clear to the throng outside, as well. Whole minutes had gone by, and still no one mounted the veranda to seek close quarters with the farmer—who stood braced with his legs wide apart, bare-headed and erect, the wind blowing his huge beard sidewise over his shoulder.

"Well, ain't none o' you a-comin'?" he called out at last, with impatient sarcasm. "Thought you was so sot on taking me out an' having some fun with me!" After a brief pause, another taunt occurred to him. "Why, even the niggers you're so in love with," he shouted, "they ain't such dod-rotted cowards as you be!"

A general movement was discernible among the shadowy forms outside. I thought for the instant that it meant a swarming attack upon the veranda. But no! suddenly it had grown much lighter, and the mob was moving away toward the rear of the house. The men were shouting things to one another, but the wind for the moment was at such a turbulent pitch that all their words were drowned. The reddened light waxed brighter still—and now there was nobody to be seen at all from the window.

"Hurry here! Mr. Beech! *We're all afire!*" cried a frightened voice in the room behind me.

It may be guessed how I turned.

The kitchen door was open, and the figure of a woman stood on the threshold, indefinitely black against a strange yellowish-drab half light which framed it. The woman—one knew from the voice that it was Esther Hagadorn—seemed to be wringing her hands.

" Hurry ! Hurry ! " she cried again, and I could see now that the little passage was full of grey luminous smoke, which was drifting past her into the living-room. Even as I looked, it had half obscured her form, and was rolling in, in waves.

Abner had heard her, and strode across the room now, gun still in hand, into the thick of the smoke, pushing Esther before him and shutting the kitchen door with a bang as he passed through. I put in a terrified minute or two alone in the dark, amazed and half-benumbed by the confused sounds that at first came from the kitchen, and by the horrible suspense when a still more sinister silence ensued. Then there rose a loud crackling noise, like the incessant popping of some giant variety of corn. The door burst open again, and M'rye's tall form seemed literally flung into the room by the sweeping volume of dense smoke which poured in. She pulled the door to behind her—then gave a snarl of excited emotion at seeing me by the dusky reddened radiance which began forcing its way from outside through the holland window shades.

" Light the lamp, you gump ! " she commanded, breathlessly and fell with fierce concentration upon the task of dragging furniture out from the bed-room. I helped her in a frantic, bewildered fashion, after I had lighted the lamp, which flared and smoked without its shade, as we toiled. M'rye seemed all at once to have the strength of a dozen men. She swung the ponderous chest of drawers out end on end ; she fairly lifted the still bigger bookcase, after I had hustled the books out on to the table ; she swept off the bedding, slashed the cords, and jerked the bed-posts and side-pieces out of their connecting sockets with furious energy, till it seemed as if both rooms must have been dismantled in less time than I have taken to tell of it.

The crackling overhead had swollen now to a wrathful roar, rising above the gusty voices of the wind. The noise, the heat, the smoke, and terror of it all made me sick and faint. I grew dizzy, and did foolish things in an aimless way, fumbling about among the stuff M'rye was hurling forth. Then all at once her darkling, smoke-wrapped figure shot up to an enormous height, the lamp began to go round, and I felt myself with nothing but space under my feet, plunging downward with awful velocity, surrounded by whirling skies full of stars.

There was a black night-sky overhead when I came to my senses again, with flecks of snow in the cold air on my face. The wind had fallen, everything was as still as death, and some one was carrying me in his arms. I tried to lift my head.

"Aisy now!" came Hurley's admonitory voice, close to my ear. "We'll be there in a minyut."

"No—I'm all right—let me down," I urged. He set me on my feet, and I looked amazedly about me.

The red-brown front of our larger hay-barn loomed in a faint unnatural light, at close quarters, upon my first inquiring gaze. The big sliding-doors were open, and the slanting waggon-bridge running down from their threshold was piled high with chairs, bedding, crockery, milk-pans, clothing—the jumbled remnants of our household gods. Turning, I looked across the yard upon what was left of the Beech homestead—a glare of cherry light glowing above a fiery hole in the ground.

Strangely enough this glare seemed to perpetuate in its outlines the shape and dimensions of the vanished house. It was as if the house were still there, but transmuted from joists and clapboards and shingles, into an illuminated and impalpable ghost of itself. There was a weird effect of transparency about it. Through the spectral bulk of red light I could see the naked and gnarled apple-trees in the home-orchard on the further side ; and I remembered at once that painful and striking parallel of Scrooge gazing through the re-edified body of Jacob Marley, and beholding the buttons at the back of his coat. It all seemed some monstrous dream.

But no, here the others were. Janey Wilcox and the Underwood girl had come out from the barn, and were carrying in more things. I perceived now that there was a candle burning inside, and presently Esther Hagadorn was to be seen. Hurley had disappeared, and so I went up the sloping platform to join the women—noting with weak surprise that my knees seemed to have acquired new double-joints and behaved as if they were going in the other direction. I stumbled clumsily once I was inside the barn, and sat down with great abruptness on a milking-stool, leaning my head back against the hay mow, and conscious of entire indifference as to whether school kept or not.

Again it was like some half-waking vision— the feeble light of the candle losing itself upon the broad high walls of new hay ; the huge shadows in the rafters overhead ; the women-folk silently moving about, fixing up on the barn floor some pitiful imitation, poor souls, of the home that had been swept off the face of the earth, and outside, through the wide sprawling doors, the dying away effulgence of the embers of our roof-tree lingering in the air of the winter night.

Abner Beech came in presently, with the gun in one hand, and a blackened and outlandish-looking object in the other, which turned out to be the big pink sea-shell that used to decorate the parlour mantel. He held it up for M'rye to see, with a grave, tired smile on his face.

"We got it out, after all—just by the skin of our teeth," he said, and Hurley, behind him, confirmed this by an eloquent grimace.

M'rye's black eyes snapped and sparkled as she lifted the candle and saw what this something was. Then she boldly put up her face and kissed her husband with a resounding smack. Truly it was a night of surprises.

"That's about the only thing I had to call my own when I was married," she offered in explanation of her fervour, speaking to the company at large. Then she added in a lower tone, to Esther: "*He* used to play with it for hours at a stretch—when he was a baby."

"Remember how he used to hold it up to his ear, eh, mother?" asked Abner, softly.

M'rye nodded her head, and then put her apron up to her eyes for a brief moment. When she lowered it, we saw an unaccustomed smile mellowing her hard-set, swarthy face.

The candle light flashed upon a tear on her cheek that the apron had missed.

" I guess I *do* remember ! " she said, with a voice full of tenderness.

Then Esther's hand stole into M'rye's and the two women stood together before Abner, erect and with beaming countenances, and he smiled upon them both.

It seemed that we were all much happier in our minds, now that our house had been burned down over our heads.

## XI

SOME time during the night I was awakened by the mice frisking through the hay about my ears. My head was aching again, and I could not get back into sleep. Besides, Hurley was snoring mercilessly.

We two had chosen for our resting-place the little mow of half a load or so, which had not been stowed away above, but lay ready for present use over by the side-door opening on the cow-yard. Temporary beds had been spread for the women with fresh straw and blankets at the further end of the central threshing-floor. Abner himself had taken one of the rescued ticks and a quilt over to the other end, and stretched his ponderous length out across the big doors, with the gun by his side. No one had, of course, dreamed of undressing.

Only a few minutes of wakefulness sufficed to throw me into a desperate state of fidgets. The hay seemed full of strange creeping noises. The whole big barn echoed with the boisterous ticking of the old eight-day clock which had been saved from the wreck of the kitchen, and which M'rye had set going again on the seat of the democrat waggon. And then Hurley!

I began to be convinced, now, that I was coming down with a great spell of sickness— perhaps even " the fever." Yes, it undoubtedly was the fever. I could feel it in my bones, which now started up queer prickly sensations on novel lines, quite as if they were somebody else's bones instead. My breathing, indeed, left a good deal to be desired from the true fever stand-point. It was not nearly so rapid or convulsive as I understood that the breathing of a genuine fever victim ought to be. But that, no doubt, would come soon enough—nay! was it not already coming? I thought, upon examination, that I did breathe more swiftly than before. And oh! that Hurley!

As noiselessly as possible I made my way, half-rolling, half-sliding, off the hay, and got on my feet on the floor. It was pitch dark, but I could feel along the old disused stanchion-row to the

corner ; thence it was plain sailing over to where
Abner was sleeping by the big front doors. I
would not dream of rousing him if he was in
truth asleep, but it would be something to be nigh
him, in case the fever should take a fatal turn
before morning. I would just cuddle down on
the floor near to him, and await events.

When I had turned the corner, it surprised me
greatly to see ahead of me, over at the front of
the barn, the reflection of a light. Creeping along
toward it, I came out upon Abner, seated with
his back against one of the doors, looking over an
account-book by the aid of a lantern perched on
a box at his side. He had stood the frame of an
old bob-sleigh on end close by, and hung a horse-
blanket over it, so that the light might not disturb
the women-folk at the other end of the barn.
The gun lay on the floor beside him.

He looked up at my approach, and regarded
me with something, I fancied, of disapprobation in
his habitually grave expression.

"Well, old seventy-six, what's the matter with
you ? " he asked, keeping his voice down to make
as little noise as possible.

I answered in the same cautious tones that I
was feeling bad. Had any encouragement suggested itself in the farmer's mien, I was prepared
to overwhelm him with a relation of my symp-
toms in detail. But he shook his head instead.

"You'll have to wait till morning to be sick," he said—"that is, to get 'tended to. I don't know anything about such things, an' I wouldn't wake M'rye up now for a whole baker's dozen o' you chaps." Seeing my face fall at this sweeping declaration, he proceeded to modify it in a kindlier tone. "Now you just lay down again, sonny," he added, "an' you'll be to sleep in no time, and in the morning M'rye 'll fix up something for ye. This ain't no fit time of night for white folks to be belly-achin' around."

"I kind o' thought I'd feel better if I was sleeping over here near you," I ventured now to explain, and his nod was my warrant for tiptoeing across to the heap of disorganised furniture, and getting out some blankets and a comforter, which I arranged in the corner a few yards away and simply rolled myself up in, with my face turned away from the light. It was better over here than with Hurley, and though that prompt sleep which the farmer had promised did not come, I at least was drowsily conscious of an improved physical condition.

Perhaps I drifted off more than half-way into dreamland, for it was with a start that all at once I heard some one close by talking with Abner.

"I saw you were up, Mr. Beech"—it was Esther Hagadorn who spoke—"and I don't seem able to sleep, and I thought, if you didn't mind, I'd come over here."

" Why, of course," the farmer responded. " Just bring up a chair there, an' sit down. That's it— wrap the shawl around you good. It's a cold night—snowin' hard outside."

Both had spoken in muffled tones so as not to disturb the others. This same dominant notion of keeping still deterred me from turning over, in order to be able to see them. I expected to hear them discuss my illness, but they never referred to it. Instead, there was what seemed a long silence. Then the school-ma'am spoke.

" I can't begin to tell you," she said, " how glad I am that you and your wife aren't a bit cast down by the—the calamity."

" No," came back Abner's voice, buoyant even in its half-whisper, " we're all right. I've been sort o' figuring up here, an' they ain't much real harm done. I'm insured pretty well. Of course, this bein' obleeged to camp out in a hay barn might be improved on, but then it's a change, something out o' the ordinary rut, an' it'll do us good. I'll have the carpenters over from Juno Mills in the forenoon, an' if they push things, we can have a roof over us again before Christmas. It could be done even sooner, p'raps, only they ain't any neigh- bours to help *me* with a raisin' bee. They're willin' enough to burn my house down, though. However

I don't want them not an atom more'n they want
me."

There was no trace of anger in his voice. He
spoke like one contemplating the unalterable conditions of life.

" Did they really, do you believe, *set* it on fire ? "
Esther asked, intently.

" No, *I* think it caught from that fool-fire they
started around back of the house, to heat their fool
tar by. The wind was blowing a regular gale,
you know. Janey Wilcox, she will have it that
that Roselle Upman set it on purpose. But then,
she don't like him, and I can't blame her much, for
that matter. Once Otis Barnum was seein' her
home from singin' school, an' when he was goin'
back alone this Roselle Upman waylaid him in the
dark, and pitched onto him, an' broke his collar-
bone. I always thought it puffed Janey up some,
this bein' fought over like that, but it made her
mad to have Otis hurt on her account, an' then
nothing come of it. I wouldn't a' minded pep-
perin' Roselle's legs a trifle, if I'd had a barrel
loaded, say with birdshot. He's a nuisance to the
whole neighbourhood. He kicks up a fight at
every dance he goes to, all winter long, an' hangs
around the taverns day in and day out, inducing
young men to drink and loaf. I thought a fellow
like him would be sure to go off to the war, and
so good riddance ; but no, darned if the coward

don't go and get his front teeth pulled, so that he can't bite ca'tridges, and jest stay around, a worse nuisance than ever. I'd half forgive that miserable war if it only took off the—the right men."

"Mr. Beech," said Esther, in low fervent tones, measuring each word as it fell, "you and I, we must forgive that war together."

I seemed to see the farmer shaking his head. He said nothing in reply.

"I'm beginning to understand how you've felt about it all along," the girl went on, after a pause. "I knew the fault must be in my ignorance, that our opinions of plain right and plain wrong should be such poles apart. I got a school-friend of mine, whose father is your way of thinking, to send me all the papers that came to their house, and I've been going through them religiously— whenever I could be quite alone. I don't say I don't think you're wrong, because I *do*, but I am getting to understand how you should believe yourself to be right."

She paused as if expecting a reply, but Abner only said, "Go on," after some hesitation, and she went on :

"Now take the neighbours all about here——"

"Excuse *me !*" broke in the farmer. "I guess if it's all the same to you, I'd rather not. They're too rich for my blood."

"Take these very neighbours," pursued Esther,

with gentle determination.   " Something must be
very wrong indeed when they behave to you the
way they do.   Why, I know that even now, right
down in their hearts, they recognise that you're
far and away the best man in Agrippa.   Why, I
remember, Mr. Beech, when I first applied, and
you were school-commissioner, and you sat there
through the examination—why, you were the
only one whose opinion I gave a rap for.   When
you praised me, why, I was prouder of it than
if you had been a Regent of the University.
And I tell you, everybody all around here feels at
bottom just as I do."

" They take a dummed curious way of showing
it, then," commented Abner, roundly.

" It isn't *that* they're trying to show at all,"
said Esther.   " They feel that other things are
more important.   They're all wrought up over
the war.   How could it be otherwise when almost
every one of them has got a brother, or a father,
or—or—*a son*—down there in the South, and every
day brings news that some of these have been
shot dead, and môre still wounded and crippled,
and others—*others*, that God only knows *what*
has become of them—oh, how can they help
feeling that way?   I don't know that I ought
to say it—" the school-ma'am stopped to catch
her breath, and hesitated, then went on—" but
yes, you'll understand me *now*—there was a time

here, not so long ago, Mr. Beech, when I downright hated you—you and M'rye both!"

This was important enough to turn over for.
I flopped as unostentatiously as possible, and
neither of them gave any sign of having noted my
presence. The farmer sat with his back against
the door, the quilt drawn up to his waist, his
head bent in silent meditation. His whole profile
was in deep shadow from where I lay—darkly
massive and powerful and solemn. Esther was
watching him with all her eyes, leaning forward
from her chair, the lantern-light full upon her
eager face.

"M'rye and I don't lay ourselves out to be specially bad folks, as folks go," the farmer said at last,
by way of deprecation. "We've got our faults, of
course, like the rest, but——"

"No," interrupted Esther, with a half-tearful
smile in her eyes. "You only pretend to have
faults. You really haven't got any at all."

The shadowed outline of Abner's face softened.
"Why, that *is* a fault itself, ain't it?" he said, as
if pleased with his logical acuteness.

The crowing of some foolish rooster, grown
tired of waiting for the belated November daylight,
fell upon the silence from one of the buildings
near by.

Abner Beech rose to his feet with ponderous
slowness, pushing the bedclothes aside with his

I

boot, and stood beside Esther's chair. He laid his big hand on her shoulder with a patriarchal gesture.

"Come now," he said, gently, "you go back to bed, like a good girl, an' get some sleep. It'll be all right."

The girl rose in turn, bearing her shoulder so that the fatherly hand might still remain upon it. "Truly?" she asked, with a new light upon her pale face.

"Yes—truly!" Abner replied, gravely nodding his head.

Esther took the hand from her shoulder, and shook it in both of hers. "Good-night again, then," she said, and turned to go.

Suddenly there resounded the loud rapping of a stick on the barn door, close by my head.

Abner squared his huge shoulders and threw a downright glance at the gun on the floor.

"Well?" he called out.

"*Is my da'ater inside there?*"

We all knew that thin, high-pitched, querulous voice. It was old "Jee" Hagadorn who was outside.


## XII


ABNER and Esther stood for a bewildered minute, staring at the rough unpainted boards through

which this astonishing inquiry had come. I
scrambled to my feet and kicked aside the tick
and blankets. Whatever else happened, it did
not seem likely that there was any more sleeping
to be done. Then the farmer strode forward and
dragged one of the doors back on its squeaking
rollers. Some snow fell in upon his boots from
the ridge that had formed against it overnight.
Save for a vaguely faint snow-light in the air, it
was still dark.

"Yes, she's here," said Abner, with his hand on
the open door.

" Then I'd like to know——" the invisible Jee
began excitedly shouting from without.

"Sh-h! You'll wake everybody up!" the farmer
interposed. " Come inside, so that I can shut the
door."

"Never under your roof!" came back the shrill
hostile voice. " I swore I never would, and I
won't ! "

" You'd have to take a crowbar to get under
my ordinary roof," returned Abner, grimly conscious of a certain humour in the thought. " What's
left of it is layin' over yonder in what used to be
the cellar. So you needn't stand on ceremony
on *that* account. I ain't got no house now, so
your oath ain't binding. Besides, the Bible says,
' Swear not at all ! ' "

A momentary silence ensued ; then Abner

rattled the door on its wheels. "Well, what are you goin' to do" he asked, impatiently. "I can't keep this door open all night, freezing everybody to death. If you won't come in, you'll have to stay out!" and again there was an ominous creaking of the rollers.

"I want my da'ater?" insisted Jehoiada, vehemently. "I stand on a father's rights."

"A father ain't got no more rights to make a fool of himself than anybody else," replied Abner, gravely. "What kind of a time of night is this, with the snow knee-deep, for a girl to be out of doors? She's all right here, with my women-folks, an' I'll bring her down with the cutter in the mornin'—that is, if she wants to come. And now, once for all, will you step inside or not?"

Esther had taken up the lantern and advanced with it now to the open door. "Come in, father," she said, in tones which seemed to be authoritative. "They've been very kind to me. Come in!"

Then, to my surprise, the lean and scrawny figure of the cooper emerged from the darkness, and, stepping high over the snow, entered the barn, Abner sending the door to behind him with a mighty sweep of the arm.

Old Hagadorn came in grumbling under his breath, and stamping the snow from his feet with sullen kicks. He bore a sledge-stake in one of his mittened hands. A worsted comforter was

wrapped around his neck and ears and partially
over his conical-peaked cap. He rubbed his long
thin nose against his mitten and blinked sulkily
at the lantern and the girl who held it.

"So here you be!" he said at last, in vexed
tones. "And me traipsing around in the snow
the best part of the night looking for you!"

"See here, father," said Esther, speaking in a
measured, deliberate way, "we won't talk about
that at all. If a thousand times worse things had
happened to both of us than have, it still wouldn't
be worth mentioning compared with what has
befallen these good people here. They've been
attacked by a mob of rowdies and loafers, and had
their house and home burned down over their
heads and been driven to take refuge here in this
barn of a winter's night. They've shared their
shelter with me and been kindness itself, and now
that you're here, if you can't think of anything
pleasant to say to them, if I were you I'd say nothing at all."

This was plain talk, but it seemed to produce a
satisfactory effect upon Jehoiada. He unwound
his comforter enough to liberate his straggling
sandy beard and took off his mittens. After a
moment or two he seated himself in the chair,
with a murmured "I'm jest about tuckered out,"
in apology for the action. He did, in truth, present a woful picture of fatigue and physical feeble-

ness, now that we saw him in repose. The bones seemed ready to start through the parchment-like skin on his gaunt cheeks, and his eyes glowed with an unhealthy fire, as he sat, breathing hard and staring at the jumbled heaps of furniture on the floor.

Esther had put the lantern again on the box and drawn forward a chair for Abner, but the farmer declined it with a wave of the hand and continued to stand in the background, looking his ancient enemy over from head to foot with a meditative gaze. Jehoiada grew visibly nervous under this inspection ; he fidgeted on his chair and then fell to coughing—a dry, rasping cough which had an evil sound, and which he seemed to make the worse by fumbling aimlessly at the button that held the overcoat collar round his throat.

At last Abner walked slowly over to the shadowed masses of piled-up household things, and lifted out one of the drawers that had been taken from the framework of the bureau and brought over with their contents. Apparently it was not the right one, for he dragged aside a good many objects to get at another, and rummaged about in this for several minutes. Then he came out again into the small segment of the lantern's radiance with a pair of long thick woollen stockings of his own in his hand.

"You better pull off them wet boots and draw

these on," he said, addressing Hagadorn, but looking fixedly just over his head. " It won't do that
cough o' yours no good, settin' around with wet
feet."

The cooper looked in a puzzled way at the huge
butternut-yarn stockings held out under his nose,
but he seemed too much taken aback to speak or
to offer to touch them.

" Yes, father ! " said Esther, with quite an air of
command. " You know what that cough means,"
and straightway Hagadorn lifted one of his feet
to his knee and started tugging at the boot-heel in
a desultory way. He desisted after a few half-
hearted attempts, and began coughing again, this
time more distressingly than ever.

His daughter sprang forward to help him, but
Abner pushed her aside, put the stockings under
his arm, and himself undertook the job. He did
not bend his back overmuch, but hoisted Jee's foot
well in the air and pulled.

" Brace your foot agin mine an' hold on to the
chair ! " he ordered, sharply, for the first effect of
his herculean pull had been to nearly drag the
cooper to the floor. He went at it more gently
now, easing the soaked leather up and down over
the instep until the boots were off. He looked
furtively at the bottoms of these before he tossed
them aside, noting, no doubt, as I did, how old
and broken and run down at the heel they were.

Jee himself peeled off the drenched stockings, and they too were flimsy old things, darned and mended almost out of their original colour.

These facts served only to deepen my existing low opinion of Hagadorn, but they appeared to affect Abner Beech differently. He stood by and watched the cooper dry his feet and then draw on the warm dry hose over his shrunken shanks, with almost a friendly interest. Then he shoved along one of the blankets across the floor to Hagadorn's chair that he might wrap his feet in it.

" That's it," he said, approvingly. " They ain't no means of building a fire here right now, but as luck would have it we'd jest set up an old kitchen stove in the little cow-barn to warm up gruel for the ca'aves with, an' the first thing we'll do'll be to rig it up in here to cook breakfast by, an' then we'll dry them boots o' yourn in no time. You go an' pour some oats into 'em now," Abner added, turning to me. " And you might as well call Hurley. We've got considerable to do, and daylight's breakin'."

The Irishman lay on his back where I had left him, still snoring tempestuously. As a rule he was a light sleeper, but this time I had to shake him again and again before he understood that it was morning. I opened the side-door, and sure enough, the day had begun. The clouds had cleared away. The sky was still ashen-grey overhead, but

the light from the horizon, added to the whiteness
of the unaccustomed snow, rendered it quite easy
to see one's way about inside.    I went to the oat-
bin.

Hurley, sitting up and rubbing his eyes, regarded me and my task with curiosity.    " An' is
it a stove-pipe for a measure ye have ?" he
asked.

" No ; it's one of Jee Hagadorn's boots," I replied.    " I'm filling 'em so that they'll swell when
they're dryin'."

He slid down off the hay as if some one had
pushed him.    " What's that ye say ?    Haggydorn ?
*Ould* Haggydorn ? " he demanded.

I nodded assent.    " Yes, he's inside with Abner,"
I explained.    " An' he's got on Abner's stockin's,
an' it looks like he's going to stay to breakfast."

Hurley opened his mouth in sheer surprise and
gazed at me with hanging jaw and round eyes.

" 'Tis the fever that's on ye," he said, at last.
" Ye're wanderin' in yer mind ! "

" You just go in and see for yourself," I replied,
and Hurley promptly took me at my word.

He came back presently, turning the corner of
the stanchions in a depressed and rambling way,
quite at variance with his accustomed swinging
gait.    He hung his head, too, and shook it over
and over again perplexedly.

" Abner and me'll be bringin' in the stove," he

said.   "'Tis not fit for you to go out wid that
sickness on ye."

"Well, anyway," I retorted, "you see I wasn't
wanderin' much in my mind."

Hurley shook his head again.   "Well, then,"
he began, lapsing into deep brogue and speaking
rapidly, "I've meself seen the woman wid the
head of a horse on her in the lake forninst the
Three Castles, an' me sister's first man, sure he
broke down the ditch round about the Danes' fort
on Dunkelly, an' a foine grand young man, small
for his strength an' wid a red cap on his head,
flew out an' wint up in the sky, an' whin he related
it up comes Father Forrest to him in the potaties,
an' says he, 'I do be surprised wid you, O'Driscoll,
for to be relatin' such loies.'   'I'll take me Bible
oat' on 'em !' says he.   "'Tis your imagination !'
says the priest.   'No imagination at all !' says
O'Driscoll ; 'sure, I saw it wid dese two eyes, as
plain as I'm lookin' at your riverence, an' a far
grander sight it was too !'   An' me own mother,
faith, manny's the toime I've seen her makin' up
dhrops for the yellow sickness wid woodlice, an'
sayin' Hail Marys over 'em, an' thim same 'ud cure
annything from sore teeth to a wooden leg for
moiles round.   But, saints help me !   I never seen
the loikes o' *this !*   Haggydorn is it ?   *Ould* Haggydorn !   *Huh !*"

Then the Irishman, still with a dejected air,

started off across the yard through the snow to the cow-barns, mumbling to himself as he went.

I had heard Abner's heavy tread coming along the stanchions toward me, but now all at once it stopped. The farmer's wife had followed him into the passage, and he had halted to speak with her.

"They ain't no two ways about it, mother," he expostulated. "We jest got to put the best face on it we kin, and act civil, an' pass the time o' day as if nothing 'd ever happened atween us. He'll be goin' the first thing after breakfast."

"Oh! I ain't agoin' to sass him, or say anything uncivil," M'rye broke in, reassuringly. "What I mean is, I don't want to come into the for'ard end of the barn at all. They ain't no need of it. I kin cook the breakfast in back, and Janey kin fetch it for'ard for ye, an' nobody need say anythin', or be any the wiser."

"Yes, I know," argued Abner, "but there's the looks o' the thing. *I* say, if you're goin' to do a thing, why, do it right up to the handle, or else don't do it at all. An' then there's the girl to consider, and *her* feelin's."

"Dunno't her feelin's are such a pesky sight more importance than other folkses," remarked M'rye, callously.

This unaccustomed recalcitrancy seemed to take Abner aback. He moved a few steps forward, so that he became visible from where I stood, then halted again and turned, his shoulders rounded, his hands clasped behind his back. I could see him regarding M'rye from under his broad hat brim with a gaze at once dubious and severe.

" I ain't much in the habit o' hearin' you talk this way to me, mother," he said at last, with grave depth of tones and significant deliberation.

" Well, I can't help it, Abner," rejoined M'rye, bursting forth in vehement utterance, all the more excited from the necessity she felt of keeping it out of hearing of the unwelcome guest. " I don't want to do anything to aggravate you, or go contrary to your notions, but with even the willingest pack-horse there *is* such a thing as piling it on too thick. I can stand bein' burnt out o' house 'n' home, an' seeing pretty nigh every rag and stick I had in the world go kitin' up the chimney, and campin' out here in a barn—My Glory, yes !—and as much more on top o' that ; but, I tell you flat-footed, I can't stomach Jee Hagadorn, an' I *won't !*"

Abner continued to contemplate the revolted M'rye with displeased amazement written all over his face. Once or twice I thought he was going to speak, but nothing came of it. He only looked and looked as if he had the greatest difficulty in crediting what he saw.

Finally, with a deep-chested sigh, he turned again. " I s'pose this is still more or less of a free country," he said. "If you're sot on it, I can't hender you," and he began walking once more toward me.

M'rye followed him out and put a hand on his arm. "Don't go off like that, Abner," she adjured him. "You *know* there ain't nothin' in this whole wide world I wouldn't do to please you—if I *could*. But this thing jest goes ag'in' my grain. It's the way folks are made. It's your nater to be forgivin' an' do good to them that despitefully use you."

"No, it ain't," declared Abner, vigorously. "No, sirree! 'Hold fast!' is my nater. I stand out ag'in' my enemies till the last horn blows. But when they come wadin' in through the snow, with their feet sopping wet and coughing fit to turn themselves inside out, and their daughter is there, and you've sort o' made it up with her, and we're all camping out in a barn, don't you see——"

"No, I can't see it," replied M'rye, regretful but firm. "They always said we Ramswells had Injun blood in us somewhere. An' when I get an Injun streak on me, right down in the marrow o' my bones, why, you mustn't blame me, or feel hard if, if—I——"

"No-o," said Abner, with reluctant conviction, "I s'pose not. I daresay you're acting accordin' to your lights. An' besides, he'll be going the first thing after breakfast."

" And you ain't mad, Abner ? " pleaded M'rye, almost tremulously, as if frightened at the dimensions of the victory she had won."

" Why, bless your heart, no," answered the farmer, with a glaring simulation of easy-mindedness.   " No—that's all right, mother ! "

Then with long heavy-footed strides the farmer marched past me and out into the cow-yard.


## XIII

IF there was ever a more curious meal in Dearborn County than that first breakfast of ours in the barn, I never heard of it.

The big table was among the things saved from the living-room, and Esther spread it again with the cloth which had been in use on the previous evening.   There was the stain of the tea which the Underwood girl had spilled in the excitement of the supper's rough interruption ; there were other marks of calamity upon it as well—the smudge of cinders, for one thing, and a general diffused effect of smokiness.   But it was the only table-cloth we had.   The dishes, too, were a queer lot, representing two or three sets of widely differing patterns and value, other portions of which we should never see again.

When it was announced that breakfast was

ready, Abner took his accustomed armchair at
the head of the table. He only half turned his
head toward Hagadorn and said, in formal tones,
over his shoulder, " Won't you draw up and have
some breakfast ? "

Jee was still sitting where he had planted himself two hours or so before. He still wore his
round cap, with the tabs tied down over his ears.
In addition to his overcoat, some one—probably
his daughter—had wrapped a shawl about his
thin shoulders. The boots had not come in, as
yet, from the stove, and the blanket was drawn up
over his stockinged feet to the knees. From
time to time his lips moved, as if he were reciting
scripture texts to himself, but, so far as I knew,
he had said nothing to any one. His cough
seemed rather worse than better.

" Yes, come, father ! " Esther added to the
farmer's invitation, and drew a chair back for
him, two plates away from Abner. Thus adjured,
he rose and hobbled stiffly over to the place indi-
cated, bringing his foot-blanket with him. Esther
stooped to arrange this for him, and then seated
herself next the host.

" You see, I'm going to sit beside you, Mr.
Beech," she said, with a wan little smile.

" Glad to have you," remarked Abner, gravely.

The Underwood girl brought in a first plate of
buckwheat cakes, set it down in front of Abner,

and took her seat opposite Hagadorn and next to me. There remained three vacant places, down at the foot of the table, and though we all began eating without comment, everybody continually encountered some other's glance straying significantly toward these empty seats. Janey Wilcox, very straight and with an uppish air, came in with another plate of cakes, and marched out again in tell-tale silence.

"Hurley! Come along in here and git your breakfast!"

The farmer fairly roared out this command, then added, in a lower, apologetic tone: "I 'spec' the women folks have got their hands full with that broken-down old stove."

We all looked toward the point, half-way down the central barn-floor, where the democrat waggon, drawn crosswise, served to divide our improvised living-room and kitchen. Through the wheels, and under its uplifted pole, we could vaguely discern two petticoated figures at the extreme other end, moving about the stove, the pipe of which was carried up and out through a little window above the door. Then Hurley appeared, ducking his head under the waggon-pole.

"I'm aitin' out here, convanient to the stove," he shouted from this dividing line.

"No, come and take your proper place," bawled back the farmer, and Hurley had nothing to do but obey. He advanced with obvious reluctance, and halted at the foot of the table, eyeing with awkward indecision the three vacant chairs. One was M'rye's ; the others would place him either next to the hated cooper or diagonally opposite, where he must look at him all the while.

"Sure, I'm better out there," he ventured to insist in a wheedling tone, but Abner thundered forth an angry "No, sir," and the Irishman sank abruptly into the seat beside Hagadorn. From this place he eyed the Underwood girl with a glare of contemptuous disapproval. I learned afterward that M'rye and Janey Wilcox regarded her desertion of them as the meanest episode of the whole miserable morning, and beguiled their labours over the stove by recounting to each other all the low-down qualities illustrated by the general history of her "sap-headed tribe."

Meanwhile conversation languished.

With the third or fourth instalment of cakes, Janey Wilcox had halted long enough to deliver herself of a few remarks, sternly limited to the necessities of the occasion. "M'rye says," she declaimed, coldly, looking the while with great fixedness at the hay wall, "if the cakes are sour she can't help it. We saved what was left over of the batter, but the Graham flour and the sody are both burnt up," and with that she stalked out again.

Not even politeness could excuse the pretence on any one's part that the cakes were *not* sour, but Abner seized upon the general subject as an opening for talk.

" Remember when I was a little shaver," he remarked, with an effort at amiability, " my sisters kicked about having to bake the cakes on account of the hot stove making their faces red and spoilin' their complexions, an' they wanted specially to go to some fandango or other, and look their pootiest, an' so father sent us boys out into the kitchen to bake 'em instid.   Old Lorenzo Dow, the Methodist preacher, was stopping over-night at our house, and mother was jest beside herself to have everything go off ship-shape—and then them cakes begun comin' in.   First my brother William, he baked one the shape of a horse, and then Josh, he made one like a jackass with ears as long as the griddle would allow of lengthwise, and I'd got jest comfortably started in on one that I begun as a pig, and then was going to alter into a ship with sails up, when father, he come out with a hold-back strap, and —well—mine never got finished to this day. Mother, she was mortified most to death, but old Dow, he jest lay back and laughed—laughed till you'd thought he'd split himself."

"It was from Lorenzo Dow's lips that I had my first awakening call unto righteousness," said

Jee Hagadorn, speaking with solemn unction in high quavering tones.

The fact that he should have spoken at all was enough to take even the sourness out of M'rye's cakes.

Abner took up the ball with solicitous promptitude. "A very great man Lorenzo Dow was—in his way," he remarked.

"By grace he was spared the shame and humiliation," said Hagadorn, lifting his voice as he went on—"the humiliation of living to see one whole branch of the Church separate itself from the rest, withdraw and call itself the Methodist Episcopal Church, South, in defence of human slavery!"

Esther, red-faced with hot embarrassment, intervened peremptorily. "How *can* you, father!" she broke in. "For all you know he might have been red-hot on that side himself. In fact, I daresay he would have been. How on earth can *you* know to the contrary, anyway?"

Jee was all excitement on the instant, at the promise of an argument. His eyes flashed; he half rose from his seat and opened his mouth to reply. So much had he to say, indeed, that the words stumbled over one another on his tongue, and produced nothing but an incoherent stammering sound, which all at once was supplanted by a violent fit of coughing. So terrible were the paroxysms of this seizure, that when they had at last spent their fury the poor man was trembling like a leaf and toppled in his chair as if about to swoon.  Esther had hovered about over him from the outset of the fit, and now looked up appealingly to Abner.  The farmer rose, walked down the table side, and gathered Jee's form up under one big engirdling arm.  Then, as the girl hastily dragged forth the tick and blankets again and spread them into the rough semblance of a bed, Abner half led, half carried the cooper over and gently laid him down thereon.  Together they fixed up some sort of pillow for him with hay under the blanket, and piled him snugly over with quilts and my comfortable.

" There—you'll be better layin' down," said Abner, soothingly.  Hagadorn closed his eyes wearily and made no answer.  They left him after a minute or two and returned to the table.

The rest of the breakfast was finished almost wholly in silence.  Every once in a while Abner and Esther would exchange looks, his gravely kind, hers gratefully contented, and these seemed really to render speech needless.  For my own part, I foresaw with some degree of depression that there would soon be no chance whatever of my securing attention in the *rôle* of an invalid, at least in this part of the barn.

Perhaps, however, they might welcome me in

the kitchen part, as a sort of home-product rival
to the sick cooper. I rose and walked languidly
out into M'rye's domain. But the two women were
occupied with a furious scrubbing of rescued pans
for the morning's milk, and they allowed me to
sit feebly down on the wood-box behind the stove
without so much as a glance of sympathy.

By-and-by we heard one of the great front
doors rolled back on its shrieking wheels and
then shut to again. Some one had entered, and
in a moment there came strange, inarticulate
sounds of voices which showed that the arrival
had created a commotion. M'rye lifted her head,
and I shall never forget the wild, expectant flashing of her black eyes in that moment of suspense.

"Come in here, mother!" we heard Abner's
deep voice call out from beyond the democrat
waggon. "Here's somebody wants to see you!"

M'rye swiftly wiped her hands on her apron
and glided rather than walked toward the forward
end of the barn. Janey Wilcox and I followed
close upon her heels, dodging together under the
waggon-pole, and emerging, breathless and wild
with curiosity, on the fringe of an excited group.

In the centre of this group, standing with a
satisfied smile on his face, his general appearance
considerably the worse for wear, but in demeanour,
to quote M'rye's subsequent phrase, "as cool as
Cuffy," was Ni Hagadorn.

## XIV

" He's all right ; you can look for him here right along now, any day ; he *was* hurt a leetle, but he's as peart an' chipper now as a blue-jay on a hick'ry limb ; yes, he's a-comin' right smack home ! "

This was the gist of the assurances which Ni vouchsafed to the first rush of eager questions —to his sister, and M'rye, and Janey Wilcox. Abner had held a little aloof, to give the weaker sex a chance. Now he reasserted himself once more : " Stand back, now, and give the young man breathin' room. Janey, hand a chair for'ard —that's it. Now set ye down, Ni, an' take your own time, an' tell us all about it. So you reely found him, eh ? "

" Pshaw ! there ain't anything to that," expostulated Ni, seating himself with nonchalance, and tilting back his chair. " *That* was easy as rollin' off a log. But what's the matter *here* ? That's what knocks me. We—that is to say, I—come up on a freight train to a ways beyond Juno Junction, an' got the conductor to slow up and let me drop off, an' footed it over the hill. It was jest about broad daylight when I turned the divide. Then I began lookin' for your house, an' I'm lookin' for it still. There's a hole out there, full o' snow an' smoke, but nary a house. How'd it happen ? "

" 'Lection bonfire—high wind—woodshed must have caught," replied Abner, sententiously. " So you reely got down South, eh ? "

" An' Siss here, too !" commented Ni, with provoking disregard for the farmer's suggestions ; " a reg'lar family party. An'—hello ! "

His roving eye had fallen upon the recumbent form on the made-up bed, under the muffling blankets, and he lifted his sandy wisps of eyebrows in inquiry.

" Sh ! It's father," explained Esther. " He isn't feeling very well. I think he's asleep."

The boy's freckled, whimsical face melted upon reflection into a distinct grin. " Why," he said, " you've been havin' a reg'lar old love-feast up here. I guess it was *that* that set the house on fire ! An' speaking o' feasts, if you've got a mouthful o' somethin' to eat handy——"

The women were off like a shot to the impromptu larder at the far end of the barn.

" Well, thin," put in Hurley, taking advantage of their absence, " an' had ye the luck to see anny rale fightin' ? "

" Never mind that," said Abner ; " when he gits around to it he'll tell us everything. But, fust of all—why, he knows what I want to hear about.'

"Why, the last time I talked with you, Abner——" Ni began, squinting up one of his eyes and giving a quaint drawl to his words.

"That's a good while ago," said the farmer, quietly.

"Things have took a change, eh?" inquired Ni.

"That's neither here nor there," replied Abner, somewhat testily. "You oughtn't to need so dummed much explainin'. I've told you what I want specially to hear. An' that's what we all want to hear."

When the women had returned, and Ni, with much deliberation, had filled both hands with selected eatables, the recital at last got under way. Its progress was blocked from time to time by sheer force of tantalising perversity on the part of the narrator, and it suffered steadily from the hitches incidental to mastication; but such as it was we listened to it with all our ears, sitting or standing about, and keeping our eyes intently upon the freckled young hero.

"It wasn't so much of a job to git down there as I'd figured on," Ni said, between mouthfuls. "I got along on freight trains—once worked my way a while on a hand-car—as far as Albany, and on down to New York on a river-boat, cheap, and then, after fooling around a few days, I hitched up with the Sanitary Commission folks, and got them to let me sail on one o' their boats round to Annapolis. I thought I was going to die most of the voyage, but I didn't, you see, and when I struck Annapolis I hung around Camp Parole there quite a spell, talking with fellers that 'd been prisoners down in Richmond and got exchanged and sent North. They said there was a whole slew of our fellers down there still that 'd been brought in after Antietam. They didn't know none o' their names, but they said they'd all be sent North in time, in exchange for Johnny Rebs that we'd captured. An' so I waited round——"

"You *might* have written!" interruped Esther, reproachfully.

"What 'd been the good o' writing? I hadn't anything to tell. Besides, writing letters is for girls. Well, one day a man came up from Libby —that's the prison at Richmond—and he said there *was* a tall feller there from York State, a farmer, and he died. He thought the name was Birch, but it might have been Beech—or Body-Maple, for that matter. I s'pose you'd like to had me write *that* home!"

"No—oh, no!" murmured Esther, speaking the sense of all the company.

"Well, then I waited some more, and kept on waitin', and then waited ag'in, until bimeby, one fine day, along comes Mr. Blue-jay himself. There he was, standing up on the paddle-box with a face on him as long as your arm, and I sung out, 'Way there, Agrippa Hill!' and he come mighty nigh falling head over heels into the water. So then he come off, an' we shook hands, an' went up to the commissioners, to see about his exchange, and —and as soon's that's fixed, and the papers drawn up all correct, why, he'll come home. And that's all there is to it."

"And even *then* you never wrote!" said Esther, plaintively.

"Hold on a minute," put in Abner. "You say he's coming home. That wouldn't be unless he was disabled. They'd keep him to fight again, till his time was up. Come, now, tell the truth—he's been hurt bad!"

Ni shook his unkempt red head. "No, no," he said. "This is how it was. Fust he was fighting in a cornfield, and him and Bi Truax, they got chased out, and lost their regiment, and got in with some other fellers, and then they all waded a creek breast-high, and had to run up a long stretch of sloping ploughed ground to capture a battery they was on top o' the knoll. But they didn't see a regiment of sharp-shooters layin' hidden behind a rail fence, and these fellers riz up all to once and give it to 'em straight, and they wilted right there, and laid down, and there they was after dusk when the rebs come out and started looking round for guns and blankets and prisoners. Most of 'em was dead, or badly hurt, but they was a few who'd simply lain there in the hollow because it'd have bin death to git up. An' Jeff was one o' *them*."

"You said yourself that he had been hurt—some," interposed M'rye, with snapping eyes.

"Jest a scratch on his arm," declared Ni. "Well, then they marched the well ones back to the rear of the reb line, and there they jest skinned 'em of everything they had—watch and jack-knife and wallet and everything—and put 'em to sleep on the bare ground. Next day they started 'em out on the march toward Richmond, and after four or five days o' that, they got to a railroad, and there was cattle cars for 'em to ride the rest o' the way in. An' that's how it was."

"No," said Abner, sternly; "you haven't told us. How badly is he hurt?"

"Well," replied Ni, "it was only a scratch, as I said, but it got worse on that march, and I s'pose it wasn't tended to anyways decently, and so—and so——"

M'rye had sprung to her feet and stood now drawn up to her full height, with her sharp nose in air as if upon some strange scent, and her eyes fairly glowing in eager excitement. All at once she made a bound past us and ran to the doors, furiously digging her fingers in the crevice between them, then, with a superb sweep of the shoulders, sending them both rattling back on their wheels with a bang.

" I knew it ! " she screamed in triumph.

We who looked out beheld M'rye's black hair and brown calico dress suddenly suffer a partial eclipse of pale blue, which for the moment seemed in some way a part of the bright winter sky beyond.    Then we saw that it was a soldier who had his arm about M'rye, and his cap bent down tenderly over the head she had laid on his shoulder.

Our Jeff had come home.

A general instinct rooted us to our places and kept us silent, the while mother and son stood there in the broad open doorway;

Then the two advanced towards us, M'rye breathing hard, and with tears and smiles struggling together on her face under the shadow of a wrathful frown.   We noted nothing of Jeff's appearance save that he had grown a big yellow beard, and seemed to be smiling.   It was the mother's distraught countenance at which we looked instead.

She halted in front of Abner, and lifted the blue cape from Jeff's left shoulder, with an abrupt gesture.

" Look there ! " she said, hoarsely.   " See what they've done to my boy ! "

We saw now that the left sleeve of Jeff's army overcoat was empty and hung pinned against his breast.    On the instant we were all swarming about him, shaking the hand that remained to him and striving against one another in a babel of questions, comments, and expressions of sympathy with his loss, and satisfaction at his return. It seemed the most natural thing in the world that he should kiss Esther Hagadorn, and that Janey Wilcox should reach up on tiptoes and kiss him. When the Underwood girl would have done the same, however, M'rye brusquely shouldered her aside.

So beside ourselves with excitement were we all, each in turn seeking to get in a word edgewise, that no one noticed the approach and entrance of a stranger, who paused just over the threshold of the barn and coughed in a loud, perfunctory way to attract our attention. I had to nudge Abner twice before he turned from where he stood at Jeff's side, with his hand on the luckless shoulder, and surveyed the new-comer.

The sun was shining so brightly on the snow outside, that it was not for the moment easy to make out the identity of this shadowed figure. Abner took a forward step or two before he recognised his visitor. It was Squire Avery, the rich man of the Corners, and justice of the peace, who had once even run for Congress.

"How d' do?" said Abner, shading his eyes with a massive hand. "Won't you step in?"

The Squire moved forward a little and held

forth his hand, which the farmer took and shook doubtfully. We others were as silent now as the grave, feeling this visit to be even stranger than all that had gone before.

"I drove up right after breakfast, Mr. Beech," said the Squire, making his accustomed slow delivery a trifle more pompous and circumspect than usual, "to express to you the feeling of such neighbours as I have, in this limited space of time, being able to foregather with. I believe, sir, that I may speak for them all when I say that we regret, deplore, and contemplate with indignation the outrage and injury to which certain thoughtless elements of the community last night, sir, subjected you and your household."

"It's right neighbourly of you, Square, to come and say so," remarked Abner. "Won't you set down? You see, my son Jeff's jest come home from the war, and the house being burnt, and so on, we're rather upset for the minute."

The Squire put on his spectacles and smiled with surprise at seeing Jeff. He shook hands with him warmly, and spoke with what we felt to be the right feeling about that missing arm; but he could not sit down, he said. The cutter was waiting for him, and he must hurry back.

"I am glad, however," he added, "to have been the first, Mr. Beech, to welcome your brave son back, and to express to you the hope, sir, that with this additional link of sympathy between us, sir, bygones may be allowed to become bygones."

" I don't bear no ill-will," said Abner, guardedly. " I s'pose in the long run folks act pooty close to about what they think is right. I'm willin' to give 'em that credit, the same as I take to myself. They ain't been much disposition to give *me* that credit, but then, as our school-ma'am here was a saying last night, people 've been a good deal worked up about the war, having them that's close to 'em right down in the thick of it, and I dessay it was natural enough they should git hot in the collar about it. As I said afore, I don't bear no ill-will, though prob'ly I'm entitled to."

The Squire shook hands with Abner again. " Your sentiments, Mr. Beech," he said, in his stateliest manner, " do credit alike to your heart and your head. There is a feeling, sir, that this would be an auspicious occasion for you to resume sending your milk to the cheese factory."

Abner pondered the suggestion for a moment. " It would be handier," he said slowly, " but you know I ain't going to eat no humble pie. That Rod Bidwell was downright insulting to my man and me too——"

" It was all, I assure you, sir, an unfortunate misunderstanding," pursued the Squire, " and is now buried deep in oblivion. And it is further suggested that, when you have reached that stage of preparation for your new house, if you will communicate with me, the neighbours will be glad to come up and extend their assistance to you in what is commonly known as a raising-bee. They will desire, I believe, to bring with them their own provisions. And, moreover, Mr. Beech " —here the Squire dropped his oratorical voice and stepped close to the farmer—" if this thing has cramped you any, that is to say, if you find yourself in need of—of any accommodation——"

" No, nothing of that sort," said Abner. He stopped at that, and kept silence for a little, with his head down and his gaze meditatively fixed on the barn-floor. At last he raised his face and spoke again, his deep voice shaking a little in spite of himself.

" What you've said, Square, and your comin' here, has done me a lot o' good. It's pooty nigh wuth bein' burnt out for—to have this sort o' thing come on behind as an after-clap. Sometimes, I tell you, sir, I've despaired of the republic. I admit it, though it's to my shame. I've said to myself that when American citizens, born and raised right on the same hillside, got to behaving to each other in such an all-fired mean and cantankerous way, why, the hull blamed thing wasn't worth tryin' to save. But you see I was wrong—I admit I was wrong. It was jest a passing flurry— a kind o' snow-squall in haying time. All the while, right down at the bottom, their hearts was sound and sweet as a butter-nut. It fetches me—that does—it makes me prouder than ever I was before in all my born days to be an American—yes, sir—that's the way I—I feel about it."

There were actually tears in the big farmer's eyes, and he got out those finishing words of his in fragmentary gulps. None of us had ever seen him so affected before.

After the Squire had shaken hands again and started off, Abner stood at the open door, looking after him, then gazing in a contemplative general way upon all out doors. The vivid sunlight reflected up from the melting snow made his face to shine as if from an inner radiance. He stood still and looked across the yards, with their piles of wet straw smoking in the forenoon heat, and the black puddles eating into the snow as the thaw went on ; over the farther prospect, made weirdly unfamiliar by the disappearance of the big old farm-house ; down the long broad sloping hillside with its winding road, its checkered irregular patches of yellow stubble and stacked fodder, of deep-umber ploughed land and warm grey woodland, all pushing aside their premature mantle of sparkling white ; and the scattered homesteads and red barns beyond : and there was in his eyes the far-away look of one who saw still other things.

He turned at last and came in, walking over to where Jeff and Esther stood, hand in hand, beside the bed on the floor. Old Jee Hagadorn was sitting up now, and had exchanged some words with the couple.

"Well, Brother Hagadorn," said the farmer, "I hope you're feelin' better."

"Yes, a good deal, P—Brother Beech, thank'ee," replied the cooper, slowly and with hesitation.

Abner laid a fatherly hand on Esther's shoulder and another on Jeff's. A smile began to steal over his big face, broadening the square which his mouth cut down into his beard, and deepening the pleasant wrinkles about his eyes. He called M'rye over to the group with a beckoning nod of the head.

"It's jest occurred to me, mother," he said with the mock gravity of tone we once had known so well and of late had heard so little, "I've jest been thinking we might 'a' killed two birds with one stun while the Square was up here. He's justice of the peace, you know, an' they say them kind o' marriages turn out better'n all the others."

"Go 'long with ye," said M'rye, vivaciously. But she too put a hand on Esther's other shoulder.

The school-teacher nestled against M'rye's side. "I tell you what," she said softly, "if Jeff ever turns out to be half the man his father is, I'll just be prouder than my skin can hold,"

THE WAR WIDOW

# THE WAR WIDOW

## I

ALTHOUGH we had been one man short all day, and there was a plain threat of rain in the hot air, everybody left the hayfield long before sundown. It was too much to ask of human nature to stay off up in the remote meadows, when such remarkable things were happening down around the house.

Marcellus Jones and I were in the pasture, watching the dog get the cows together for the homeward march. He did it so well and, withal, so willingly, that there was no call for us to trouble ourselves in keeping up with him. We waited instead at the open bars until the hay-waggon had passed through, rocking so heavily in the ancient pitch-hole as it did so that the driver was nearly thrown off his perch on the top of the high load. Then we put up the bars, and fell in close behind the hay-makers. A rich cloud of dust far ahead on the road suggested that the dog was doing his work even too willingly, but for the once we feared no rebuke. Almost anything might be condoned that day.

Five grown-up men walked abreast down the highway, in the shadow of the towering waggon mow, clad much alike in battered straw hats, grey woollen shirts open at the neck, and rough old trousers bulging over the swollen, creased ankles of thick boots. One had a scythe on his arm ; two others bore forks over their shoulders. By request, Hi Tuckerman allowed me to carry his sickle.

Although my present visit to the farm had been of only a few days' duration—and those days of strenuous activity darkened by a terrible grief—I had come to be very friendly with Mr. Tuckerman. He took a good deal more notice of me than the others did ; and, when chance and leisure afforded, addressed the bulk of his remarks to me. This favouritism, though it fascinated me, was not without its embarrassing side. Hi Tuckerman had taken part in the battle of Gaines' Mill two years before, and had been shot straight through the tongue. One could still see the deep scar on each of his cheeks, a sunken and hairless pit in among his sandy beard. His heroism in the war,

and his good qualities as a citizen, had earned for
him the esteem of his neighbours, and they saw to
it that he never wanted for work. But their present respect for him stopped short of the pretence
that they enjoyed hearing him talk. Whenever
he attempted conversation, people moved away,
or began boisterous dialogues with one another to
drown him out. Being a sensitive man, he had
come to prefer silence to these rebuffs among
those he knew. But he still had a try at the occasional polite stranger—and I suppose it was in
this capacity that I won his heart. Though I
never of my own initiative understood a word he
said, Marcellus sometimes interpreted a sentence
or so for me, and I listened to all the rest with a
fraudulently wise face. To give only a solitary
illustration of the tax thus levied on our friendship, I may mention that when Hi Tuckerman
said "*Aah!*-ah-*aah*!-uh," he meant "Rappahannock," and he did this rather better than a good
many other words.

"Rappahannock," alas! was a word we heard
often enough in those days, along with Chicka-
hominy and Rapidan, and that odd Chattahoochee,
the sound of which raised always in my boyish
mind the notion that the geography-makers must
have achieved it in their baby-talk period. These
strange Southern river names, and many more,
were as familiar to the ears of these four other

untravelled Dearborn County farmers as the noise
of their own shallow Nedahma rattling over its
pebbles in the valley yonder. Only when their
slow fancy fitted substance to these names they
saw in mind's eye dark, sinister, swampy currents,
deep and silent and discoloured with human
blood.

Two of these men who strode along behind the
waggon were young half-uncles of mine, Myron
and Warren Turnbull, stout, thick-shouldered,
honest fellows not much out of their teens, who
worked hard, said little, and were always lumped
together in speech by their family, the hired help,
and the neighbours as "the boys." They asserted
themselves so rarely, and took everything as it
came with such docility, that I myself, being in
my eleventh year, thought of them as very
young indeed. Next them walked a man, hired
just for the haying, named Philleo, and then,
scuffling along over the uneven humps and hollows
on the outer edge of the road, came Si Hummaston, with the empty ginger-beer pail knocking
against his knees.

As Tuckermann's "Hi" stood for Hiram, so
I assume the other's "Si" meant Silas, or possibly
Cyrus. I daresay no one, not even his mother,
had ever called him by his full name. I know
that my companion, Marcellus Jones, who wouldn't
be thirteen until after Thanksgiving, habitually

addressed him as Si, and almost daily I resolved
that I would do so myself. He was a man
of more than fifty, I should think, tall, lean, and
what Marcellus called " bible-backed." He had
a short iron-grey beard and long hair. Whenever there was any very hard or steady work
going, he generally gave out and went to sit in
the shade, holding a hand flat over his heart, and
shaking his head dolefully. This kept a good
many from hiring him, and even in haying-time,
when everybody on two legs is of some use, I
fancy he would often have been left out if it
hadn't been for my grandparents. They respected him on account of his piety and his
moral character, and always had him down when
extra work began. He was said to be the only
hired man in the township who could not be
goaded in some way into swearing. He looked
at one slowly, with the mild expression of a heifer
calf.

We had come to the crown of the hill, and the
waggon started down the steeper incline, with a
great groaning of the brake. The men, by
some tacit understanding, halted and overlooked
the scene.

The big old stone farmhouse—part of which is
said to date almost to the Revolutionary times—
was just below us,.so near, indeed, that Marcellus
said he had once skipped a scaling-stone from where

we stood to its roof.    The dense, big-leafed foliage of a sap-bush, sheltered in the basin which dipped from our feet, pretty well hid this roof now from · view.   Further on, heavy patches of a paler, brighter green marked the orchard, and framed one side of a cluster of barns and stables, at the end of which three or four belated cows were loitering by the trough.   It was so still that we could hear the clatter of the stanchions as the rest of the herd sought their places inside the milking-barn.

The men, though, had no eyes for all this, but bent their gaze fixedly on the road, down at the bottom.   For a long way this thoroughfare was bordered by a row of tall poplars, which, as we were placed, receded from the vision in so straight a line that they seemed one high, fat tree. Beyond these one saw only a line of richer green, where the vine-wrapped rail-fences cleft their way between the ripening fields.

" I'd a' took my oath it was them," said Philleo. "I can spot them greys as fur's I can see 'em. They turned by the school-house, there, or I'll eat it, school-ma'am 'n' all.   And the buggy was follerin' 'em too."

" Yes, I thought it was them," said Myron, shading his eyes with his brown hand.

" But they ought to got past the poplars by this time, then," remarked Warren.

"Why, they'll be drivin' as slow as molasses in January," put in Si Hummaston. "When you come to think of it, it *is* pretty nigh the same as a regular funeral. You mark my words, your father 'll have walked them greys every step of the road. I s'pose he'll drive himself—he wouldn't trust bringin' Alvy home to nobody else, would he? I know I wouldn't, if the Lord had given *me* such a son; but then He didn't!"

"No, He didn't!" commented the first speaker, in an unnaturally loud tone of voice, to break in upon the chance that Hi Tuckerman was going to try to talk. But Hi only stretched out his arm, pointing the forefinger toward the poplars.

Sure enough, something was in motion down at the base of the shadows on the road. Then it crept forward, out in the sunlight, and separated itself into two vehicles. A farm waggon came first, drawn by a team of grey horses. Close after it followed a buggy, with its black top raised. Both advanced so slowly that they seemed scarcely to be moving at all.

"Well, I swan!" exclaimed Si Hummaston, after a minute, "it's Dana Pillsbury drivin' the waggon after all! Well—I dunno—yes, I guess that's prob'bly what I'd 'a' done too, if I'd be'n your father. Yes, it does look more correct, his follerin' on behind, like that. I s'pose that's Alvy's widder in the buggy there with him."

" Yes, that's Serena—it looks like her little girl with her," said Myron, gravely.

" I s'pose we might 's well be movin' along down," observed his brother, and at that we all started.

We walked more slowly now, matching our gait to the snail-like progress of those coming toward us. As we drew near to the gate, the three hired men instinctively fell behind the brothers, and in that position the group halted on the grass, facing our drive way where it left the main road. Not a word was uttered by any one. When at last the waggon came up, Myron and Warren took off their hats, and the others followed suit, all holding them poised at the level of their shoulders.

Dana Pillsbury, carrying himself rigidly upright on the box-seat, drove past us with eyes fixed straight ahead, and a face as coldly expression-less as that of a wooden Indian. The waggon was covered all over with rubber blankets, so that whatever it bore was hidden. Only a few paces behind came the buggy, and my grandfather, old Arphaxed Turnbull, went by in his turn with the same averted, far-away gaze, and the same reso-lutely stolid countenance. He held the restive young carriage horse down to a decorous walk, a single firm hand on the tight reins, without so much as looking at it. The strong yellow light of the declining sun poured full upon his long grey beard, his shaven upper lip, his dark-skinned, lean, domineering face—and made me think of some hard and gloomy old Prophet seeing a vision in the back part of the Old Testament. If that woman beside him, swathed in heavy black raiment, and holding a child up against her arm, was my Aunt Serena, I should never have guessed it.

We put on our hats again, and walked up the drive-way with measured step behind the carriage till it stopped at the side-piazza stoop. The waggon had passed on towards the big new red barn—and crossing its course I saw my Aunt Em, bareheaded and with her sleeves rolled up, going to the cow-barn with a milking-pail in her hand. She was walking quickly, as if in a great hurry.

" There's your Ma," I whispered to Marcellus, assuming that he would share my surprise at her rushing off like this, instead of waiting to say " How-d'-do " to Serena. He only nodded knowingly, and said nothing.

No one else said much of anything. Myron and Warren shook hands in stiff solemnity with the veiled and craped sister-in-law, when their father had helped her and her daughter from the buggy, and one of them remarked in a constrained way that the hot spell seemed to keep up right along. The newcomers ascended the steps to the

open door, and the woman and child went inside.
Old Arphaxed turned on the threshold, and seemed
to behold us for the first time.

" After you've put out the horse," he said, " I
want the most of yeh to come up to the new
barn.   Si Hummaston and Marcellus can do the
milkin'."

" I kind o' rinched my wrist this forenoon," put
in Si, with a note of entreaty in his voice.   He
wanted sorely to be one of the party at the red
barn.

" Mebbe milkin' 'll be good for it," said
Arphaxed, curtly.   " You and Marcellus do what
I say, and keep Sidney with you."   With this he,
too, went into the house.

II

IT wasn't an easy matter for even a member of
the family like myself to keep clearly and un-
tangled in his head all the relationships which
existed under this patriarchial Turnbull roof.

Old Arphaxed had been married twice.   His
first wife was the mother of two children, who
grew up, and the older of these was my father,
Wilbur Turnbull.   He never liked farm-life, and
left home early, not without some hard feeling,
which neither father nor son ever quite forgot.

My father made a certain success of it as a business man in Albany until, in the thirties, his health broke down. He died when I was seven, and, although he left some property, my mother was forced to supplement this help by herself going to work as forewoman in a large store. She was too busy to have much time for visiting, and I don't think there was any great love lost between her and the people on the farm ; but it was a good healthy place for me to be sent to when the summer vacation came, and withal inexpensive, and so the first of July each year generally found me out at the homestead, where, indeed, nobody pretended to be heatedly fond of me, but where I was still treated well and enjoyed myself. This year it was understood that my mother was coming out to bring me home later on.

The other child of that first marriage was a girl who was spoken of in youth as Emmeline, but whom I knew now as Aunt Em'. She was a silent, tough-fibred, hard-working creature, not at all good-looking, but relentlessly neat, and the best cook I ever knew. Even when the house was filled with extra hired men, no one ever thought of getting in any female help, so tireless and so resourceful was Em. She did all the housework there was to do, from cellar to garret, was continually lending a hand in the men's chores, made more butter than the household could eat up, managed a large kitchen-garden, and still had a good deal of spare time, which she spent in sitting out in the piazza in a starched pink calico gown, knitting the while she watched who went up and down the road. When you knew her, you understood how it was that the original Turnbulls had come into that part of the country just after the Revolution, and in a few years chopped down all the forests, dug up all the stumps, drained the swail-lands, and turned the entire place from a wilderness into a flourishing and fertile home for civilised people. I used to feel, when I looked at her that she would have been quite equal to doing the whole thing herself.

All at once, when she was something over thirty, Em had up and married a mowing-machine agent named Abel Jones, whom no one knew anything about, and who, indeed, had only been in the neighbourhood for a week or so. The family was struck dumb with amazement. The idea of Em's dallying with the notion of matrimony had never crossed anybody's mind. As a girl she had never had any patience with husking-bees or dances or sleigh-ride parties. No young man had ever seen her home from anywhere, or had had the remotest encouragement to hang around the house. She had never been pretty— so my mother told me—and as she got along in

years grew dumpy and thick in figure, with a
plain, fat face, a rather scowling brow, and an
abrupt, ungracious manner. She had no conversational gifts whatever, and through years of
increasing taciturnity and confirmed unsociability,
built up in everybody's mind the conviction that,
if there could be a man so wild and unsettled in
intellect as to suggest a tender thought to Em, he
would get his ears cuffed off his head for his
pains.

Judge, then, how like a thunderbolt the episode
of the mowing-machine agent fell upon the family.
To bewildered astonishment there soon enough
succeeded rage. This Jones was a curly-headed
man, with a crinkly black beard like those of
Joseph's brethren in the Bible picture. He had
no home and no property, and didn't seem to
amount to much even as a salesman of other
people's goods. His machine was quite the worst
then in the market, and it could not be learned
that he had sold a single one in the county. But
he had married Em, and it was calmly proposed
that he should henceforth regard the farm as his
home. After this point had been sullenly conceded, it turned out that Jones was a widower, and
had a boy nine or ten years old, named Marcellus,
who was in a sort of orphan asylum in Vermont.
There were more angry scenes between father and
daughter, and a good deal more bad blood, before

it was finally agreed that the boy also should come and live on the farm.

All this had happened in 1860 or 1861. Jones had somewhat improved on acquaintance. He knew about lightning rods, and had been able to fit out all the farm buildings with them at cost price. He had turned a little money now and again in trades with hop-poles, butter-firkins, shingles, and the like, and he was very ingenious in mending and fixing up odds and ends. He made shelves, and painted the woodwork, and put a tar roof on the summer kitchen. Even Martha, the second Mrs. Turnbull, came finally to admit that he was handy about a house.

This Martha became the head of the household while Em was still a little girl. She was a heavy woman, mentally as well as bodily, rather prone to a peevish view of things, and greatly given to pride in herself and her position, but honest, charitable in her way, and not unkindly at heart. On the whole, she was a good stepmother, and Em probably got on quite as well with her as she would have done with her own mother— even in the matter of the mowing-machine agent.

To Martha three sons were born. The two younger ones, Myron and Warren, have already been seen. The eldest boy, Alva, was the pride of the family, and for that matter, of the whole section.

Alva was the first Turnbull to go to college. From his smallest boyhood it had been manifest that he had great things before him, so handsome and clever and winning a lad was he. Through each of his schooling years he was the honour-man of his class, and he finished in a blaze of glory by taking the Clark Prize, and practically everything else within reach in the way of academic distinctions. He studied law at Octavius, in the office of Judge Schermerhorn, and in a little time was not only that distinguished man's partner, but distinctly the more important figure in the firm. At the age of twenty-five he was sent to the Assembly. The next year they made him District Attorney, and it was quite understood that it rested with him whether he should be sent to Congress later on, or be presented by the Dearborn County bar for the next vacancy on the Supreme Court bench.

At this point in his brilliant career he married Miss Serena Wadsworth, of Wadsworth's Falls. The wedding was one of the most imposing social events the county had known, so it was said, since the visit of Lafayette. The Wadsworths were an older family, even, than the Fairchilds, and infinitely more fastidious and refined. The daughters of the household, indeed, carried their refinement to such a pitch that they lived an almost solitary life, and grew to the parlous verge of oldmaidhood, simply because there was nobody good enough to marry them.  Alva Turnbull was, however, up to the standard.  It could not be said, of course, that his home surroundings quite matched those of his bride ; but, on the other hand, she was nearly two years his senior, and this was held to make matters about even.

In a year or so came the War, and nowhere in the North did patriotic excitement run higher than in this old Abolition stronghold of upper Dearborn.  Public meetings were held, and nearly a whole regiment was raised in Octavius and the surrounding towns alone.  Alva Turnbull made the most stirring and important speech at the first big gathering, and sent a thrill through the whole countryside by claiming the privilege of heading the list of volunteers.  He was made a Captain by general acclaim, and went off with his company in time to get chased from the field of Bull Run.  When he came home on a furlough in 1863 he was a Major, and later on he rose to be Lieutenant-Colonel.  We understood vaguely that he might have climbed vastly higher in promotion but for the fact that he was too moral and conscientious to get on very well with his immediate superior, General Boyce, of Thessaly, who was notoriously a drinking man.

It was glory enough to have him at the farm, on that visit of his, even as a Major.  His old parents literally abased themselves at his feet, quite tremulous in their awed pride at his greatness. It made it almost too much to have Serena there also, this fair, thin-faced, prim-spoken daughter of the Wadsworths, and actually to call her by her first name. It was haying time, I remember, but the hired men that year did not eat their meals with the family, and there was even a question whether Marcellus and I were socially advanced enough to come to the table, where Serena and her husband were feeding themselves in state with a novel kind of silver implement called a four-tined fork. If Em hadn't put her foot down, out to the kitchen we should both have gone, I fancy. As it was, we sat decorously at the far end of the table, and asked with great politeness to have things passed to us which by standing up we could have reached as well as not. It was slow, but it made us feel immensely respectable, almost as if we had been born Wadsworths ourselves.

We agreed that Serena was "stuck-up," and Marcellus reported Aunt Em as feeling that her bringing along with her a nursemaid to be waited on hand and foot, just to take care of a baby, was an imposition bordering upon the intolerable. He said that that was the sort of thing the English did until George Washington rose and drove them out. But we both felt that Alva was splendid.

He was a fine creature physically—taller even
than old Arphaxed, with huge square shoulders
and a mighty frame.    I could recall him as without whiskers, but now he had a waving, lustrous
brown beard, the longest and biggest I ever saw.
He didn't pay much attention to us boys, it was
true ; but he was affable when we came in his
way, and he gave Myron and Warren each a
dollar bill when they went to Octavius to see the
Fourth of July doings.    In the evening some of
the more important neighbours would drop in,
and then Alva would talk about the War, and
patriotism, and saving the Union, till it was like
listening to Congress itself.    He had a rich, big
voice which filled the whole room, so that the
hired men could hear every word out in the
kitchen ; but it was even more affecting to see
him walking with his father down under the
poplars, with his hands making orator's gestures
as he spoke and old Arphaxed looking at him
and listening with shining eyes.

Well, then, he and his wife went away to visit
her folks, and then we heard he had left to join
his regiment.    From time to time he wrote to
his father—letters full of high and loyal sentiments, which were printed next week in the
Octavius *Transcript*, and the week after in the
Thessaly *Banner of Liberty*.    Whenever any of
us thought about the War—and who thought

much of anything else ?—it was always with Alva as the predominant figure in every picture.

Sometimes the arrival of a letter for Aunt Em, or a chance remark about a broken chair or a clock hopelessly out of kilter, would recall for the moment the fact that Abel Jones was also at the seat of war. He had enlisted on that very night when Alva headed the roll of honour, and he had marched away in Alva's company. Somehow he got no promotion, but remained in the ranks. Not even the members of the family were shown the letters Aunt Em received, much less the printers of the newspapers. They were indeed poor misspelled scrawls, about which no one displayed any interest or questioned Aunt Em. Even Marcellus rarely spoke of his father, and seemed to share to the full the family's concentration of thought upon Alva.

Thus matters stood when Spring began to play at being Summer in the year of '64. The birds came and the trees burst forth into green, the sun grew hotter and the days longer, the strawberries hidden under the big leaves in our yard started into shape where the blossoms had been, quite in the ordinary, annual way, with us up North. But down where that dread thing they called " The War " was going on, this coming of warm weather meant more awful massacre, more tortured hearts and desolated homes than ever before.

I can't be at all sure how much later reading and
associations have helped out and patched up what
seem to be my boyish recollections of this period;
but it is, at all events, much clearer in my mind
than are the occurrences of the week before last.

We heard a good deal about how deep the mud
was in Virginia that Spring.  All the photographs
and tin-types of officers which found their way
to relatives at home now, showed them in boots
that came up to their thighs.  Everybody understood that as soon as this mud dried up a little,
there were to be most terrific doings.  The two
great lines of armies lay scowling at each other,
still on that blood-soaked fighting ground between
Washington and Richmond where they were three
years before.  Only now things were to go differently.  A new General was at the head of affairs,
and he was going in, with jaws set and nerves of
steel, to smash, kill, burn, annihilate, sparing
nothing, looking not to right or left, till the red
road had been hewed through to Richmond.  In
the first week of May this thing began—a push
forward all along the line –and the North, with
scared eyes and fluttering heart, held its breath.

My chief personal recollection of those historic
forty days is that one morning I was awakened
early by a noise in my bedroom and saw my
mother looking over the contents of the big chest
of drawers which stood against the wall.  She

was getting out some black articles of apparel. When she discovered that I was awake, she told me in a low voice that my Uncle Alva had been killed. Then a few weeks later my school closed, and I was packed off to the farm for the vacation. It will be better to tell what had happened as I learned it there from Marcellus and the others.

Along about the middle of May, the weekly paper came up from Octavius, and old Arphaxed Turnbull, as was his wont, read it over out on the piazza before supper. Presently he called his wife to him, and showed her something in it. Martha went out into the kitchen, where Aunt Em was getting the meal ready, and told her, as gently as she could, that there was very bad news for her ; in fact, her husband, Abel Jones, had been killed in the first day's battle in the Wilderness, something like a week before. Aunt Em said she didn't believe it, and Martha brought in the paper and pointed out the fatal line to her. It was not quite clear whether this convinced Aunt Em or not. She finished getting supper, and sat silently through the meal, afterwards, but she went upstairs to her room before family prayers. The next day she was about as usual, doing the work and saying nothing. Marcellus told me that to the best of his belief no one had said anything to her on the subject. The old people were a shade more ceremonious in their

manner towards her, and "the boys" and the
hired men were on the look-out to bring in water
for her from the well, and to spare her as much
as possible in the routine of chores, but no one
talked about Jones.  Aunt Em did not put on
mourning.  She made a black necktie for Marcellus to wear to church, but stayed away from
meeting herself.

A little more than a fortnight afterwards,
Myron was walking down the road from the
meadows one afternoon, when he saw a man on
horseback coming up from the poplars, galloping
like mad in a cloud of dust.  The two met at the
gate.  The man was one of the hired helps of the
Wadsworths, and he had ridden as hard as he
could pelt from the Falls, fifteen miles away, with
a message, which now he gave Myron to read.
Both man and beast dripped sweat, and trembled
with fatigued excitement.  The youngster eyed
them, and then gazed meditatively at the sealed
envelope in his hand.

"I s'pose you know what's inside?" he asked,
looking up at last.

The man in the saddle nodded, with a tell-tale
look on his face, and breathing heavily.

Myron handed the letter back, and pushed the
gate open.  "You'd better go up and give it to
father yourself," he said.  "I ain't got the heart
to face him—jest now, at any rate."

Marcellus was fishing that afternoon, over in the creek which ran through the woods. Just as at last he was making up his mind that it must be about time to go after the cows, he saw Myron sitting on a log beside the forest path, whittling mechanically, and staring at the foliage before him, in an obvious brown study. Marcellus went up to him, and had to speak twice before Myron turned his head and looked up.

" Oh! it's you, eh, Bubb?" he remarked dreamily, and began gazing once more into the thicket.

"What's the matter?" asked the puzzled boy.

" I guess Alvy's dead," replied Myron. To the lad's comments and questions he made small answer. "No," he said at last, " I don't feel much like goin' home jest now. Lea' me alone here ; I'll prob'ly turn up later on." And Marcellus went alone to the pasture, and thence, at the tail of his bovine procession, home.

When he arrived he regretted not having remained with Myron in the woods. It was like coming into something which was prison, hospital, and tomb in one. The household was paralysed with horror and fright. Martha had gone to bed, or rather had been put there by Em, and all through the night, when he woke up, he heard her broken and hysterical voice in moans and screams. The men had hitched up the greys, and Arphaxed

Turnbull was getting into the buggy to drive to Octavius for news when the boy came up. He looked twenty years older than he had at noon— all at once turned into a chalk-faced, trembling, infirm old man—and could hardly see to put his foot on the carriage-step. His son Warren had offered to go with him, and had been rebuffed almost with fierceness. Warren and the others silently bowed their heads before this mood; instinct told them that nothing but Arphaxed's show of temper held him from collapse—from falling at their feet and grovelling on the grass with cries and sobs of anguish, perhaps even dying in a fit. After he had driven off they forbore to talk to one another, but went about noiselessly with drooping chins and knotted brows.

"It jest took the tuck out of everything," said Marcellus, relating these tragic events to me. There was not much else to tell. Martha had had what they call brain-fever, and had emerged from this some weeks afterward a pallid and dim-eyed ghost of her former self, sitting for hours together in her rocking-chair in the unused parlour, her hands idly in her lap, her poor thoughts glued ceaselessly to that vague far-off Virginia which folks told about as hot and sunny, but which her mind's eye saw under the gloom of an endless and dreadful night. Arphaxed had gone South, still defiantly alone, to bring back the body of his boy. An acquaintance wrote to them of his being down sick in Washington, prostrated by the heat and strange water ; but even from his sick-bed he had sent on orders to an undertaking firm out at the front, along with a hundred dollars, their price in advance for embalming. Then, recovering, he had himself pushed down to head-quarters, or as near them as civilians might approach, only to learn that he had passed the precious freight on the way. He posted back again, besieging the railroad officials at every point with inquiries, scolding, arguing, beseeching in turn, until at last he overtook his quest at Juno Mills Junction, only a score of miles from home.

Then only he wrote, telling people his plans. He came first to Octavius, where a funeral service was held in the forenoon, with military honours, the Wadsworths as the principal mourners, and a memorable turn-out of dis-tinguished citizens. The town-hall was draped with mourning, and so was Alva's pew in the Episcopal Church, which he had deserted his ancestral Methodism to join after his marriage. Old Arphaxed listened to the novel burial service of his son's communion, and watched the clergy-man in his curious white and black vestments, with sombre pride. He himself needed and deserved only a plain and homely religion, but it was fitting that his boy should have organ music and flowers, and a ritual.

Dana Pillsbury had arrived in town early in the morning with the greys, and a neighbour's boy had brought in the buggy. Immediately after dinner Arphaxed had gathered up Alva's widow and little daughter, and started the funeral cortège upon its final homeward stage.

And so I saw them arrive on that July afternoon.

### III

FOR so good and patient a man, Si Hummaston bore himself rather vehemently during the milking. It was hotter in the barn than it was outside in the sun, and the stifling air swarmed with flies, which seemed to follow Si perversely from stall to stall and settle on his cow. One beast put her hoof square in his pail, and another refused altogether to " give down," while the rest kept up a tireless slapping and swishing of their tails very hard to bear, even if one had the help of profanity. Marcellus and I listened carefully to hear him at last provoked to an oath, but the worst thing he uttered, even when the cow stepped in the milk, was " Dum your buttons ! " which Marcellus said might conceivably be investigated by a church committee, but was hardly out-and-out swearing.

I remember Si's groans and objurgations, his querulous " Hyst there, will ye ! " his hypocritical " So-boss ! So-boss ! " his despondent " They never will give down for me ! " because presently there was crossed upon this woof of peevish impatience the web of a curious conversation.

Si had been so slow in his headway against flapping tails and restive hoofs that before he had got up to the end of the row, Aunt Em had finished her side. She brought over her stool and pail, and seated herself at the next cow to Hummaston's. For a little, one heard only the resonant din of the stout streams against the tin ; then as the bottom was covered, there came the ploughing plash of milk on milk, and Si could hear himself talk.

" S'pose you know S'reny's come, 'long with your father," he remarked, ingratiatingly.

" I saw 'em drive in," replied Em.

" *Whoa !   Hyst there !   Hole still, can't ye ?* I didn't know if you quite made out who she was, you was scootin' 'long so fast.    They ain't— *Whoa there !*—they ain't nothin' the matter 'twixt you and her, is they ? "

" I don't know as there is," said Em, curtly. " The world's big enough for both of us—we ain't no call to bunk into each other."

" No, of course—*Now you stop it !*—but it looked kind o' curious to me, your pikin off like

that, without waitin' to say 'How-d'-do?' Of
course, I never had no relation by marriage that
was stuck-up at all, or looked down on me—*Stiddy
there, now !*—but I guess I can reelize pretty
much how you feel about it. I'm a good deal
of a hand at that. It's what they call imagination.
It's a gift, you know, like good looks, or preachin',
or the knack o' makin' money. But you can't
help what you're born with, can you ? I'd been
a heap better off if my gift 'd be'n in some other
direction ; but, as I tell 'em, it ain't my fault.
And my imagination—*Hi, there! git over, will
ye ?*—it's downright cur'ous sometimes, how it
works. Now I could tell, you see, that you 'n
S'reny didn't pull together. I s'pose she never
writ a line to you, when your husband was
killed ? "

"Why should she ?" demanded Em. "We
never did correspond. What'd be the sense of
beginning then ? She minds her affairs, 'n I mind
mine. Who wanted her to write ?"

" Oh, of course not," said Si lightly. " Prob'ly
you'll git along better together, though, now that
you'll see more of one another. I s'pose S'reny's
figurin' on stayin' here right along now, her 'n'
her little girl. Well, it'll be nice for the old
folks to have somebody they're fond of. They
jest worshipped the ground Alvy walked on—and
I s'pose they won't be anything in this wide

world too good for that little girl of his.
Le's see, she must be comin' on three now, ain't
she ? "

" I don't know anything about her ! " snapped
Aunt Em, with emphasis.

" Of course, it's natural the old folks should feel
so—she bein' Alvy's child.   I hain't noticed anything special, but does it— *Well, I swan ! Hyst
there !*—does it seem to you that they're as good
to Marcellus, quite, as they used to be ?   I don't
hear 'em sayin' nothin' about his goin' to school
next winter."

Aunt Em said nothing, too, but milked doggedly
on.   Si told her about the thickness and pro-
fusion of Serena's mourning, guardedly hinted at
the injustice done him by not allowing him to go
to the red barn with the others, speculated on
the likelihood of the Wadsworths contributing to
their daughter's support, and generally exhibited
his interest in the family through a monologue
which finished only with the milking ; but Aunt
Em made no response whatever.

When the last pails had been emptied into the
big cans at the door—Marcellus and I had let
the cows out one by one into the yard, as their
individual share in the milking ended—Si and Em
saw old Arphaxed wending his way across from
the house to the red barn.   He appeared more
bent than ever but he walked with a slowness

N

which seemed born of reluctance even more than of infirmity.

"Well, now," mused Si aloud, "Brother Turnbull an' me's be'n friends for a good long spell. I don't believe he'd be mad if I cut over now to the red barn, too, seein' the milkin's all out of the way. Of course I don't want to do what ain't right—what d'you think now, Em, honest? Think it 'ud rile him?"

"I don't know anything about it?" my aunt replied with increased vigour of emphasis. "But for the land sake go somewhere! Don't hang around botherin' me. I got enough else to think of besides your everlasting cackle."

Thus rebuffed, Si meandered sadly into the cow-yard, shaking his head as he came. Seeing us seated on an upturned plough, over by the fence, from which point we had a perfect view of the red barn, he sauntered towards us, and, halting at our side, looked to see if there was room enough for him to sit also. But Marcellus, in quite a casual way, remarked: "Oh! wheeled the milk over to the house already, Si?" and at this the doleful man lounged off again in new despondency, got out the wheelbarrow, and, with ostentatious groans of travail, hoisted a can upon it and started off.

"He's takin' advantage of Arphaxed's being so worked up to play 'ole soldier' on him," said

Marcellus. "All of us have to stir him up the whole time to keep him from takin' root somewhere. I told him this afternoon 't if there had to be any settin' around under the bushes an' cryin', the fam'ly 'd do it."

We talked in hushed tones as we sat there watching the shut doors of the red barn, in boyish conjecture about what was going on behind them. I recall much of this talk with curious distinctness, but candidly it jars now upon my maturer nerves. The individual man looks back upon his boyhood with much the same amused amazement that the race feels in contemplating the memorials of its own cave-dwelling or bronze period. What strange savages we were! In those days Marcellus and I used to find our very highest delight in getting off on Thursdays, and going over to Dave Bushnell's slaughterhouse, to witness with stony hearts, and from as close a coign of vantage as might be, the slaying of some score of barnyard animals—the very thought of which now revolts our grown-up minds. In the same way we sat there on the plough, and criticised old Arphaxed's meanness in excluding us from the red barn, where the men-folks were coming in final contact with "the pride of the family." Some of the cows wandering toward us, began to "moo" with impatience for the pasture, but Marcellus said there was no hurry.

All at once we discovered that Aunt Em was standing a few yards away from us, on the other side of the fence. We could see her from where we sat by only turning a little—a motionless, stout upright figure, with a pail in her hand, and a sternly impassive look on her face. She, too, had her gaze fixed upon the red barn, and, though the declining sun was full in her eyes, seemed incapable of blinking, but just stared coldly, straight ahead.

Suddenly an unaccustomed voice fell upon our ears. Turning, we saw that a black-robed woman, with a black wrap of some sort about her head, had come up to where Aunt Em stood, and was at her shoulder. Marcellus nudged me, and whispered, " It's S'reny. Look out for squalls ! " And then we listened in silence.

" Won't you speak to me at all, Emmeline ? " we heard this new voice say.

Aunt Em's face, sharply outlined in profile against the sky, never moved. Her lips were pressed into a single line, and she kept her eyes on the barn.

" If there's anything I've done, tell me," pursued the other. " In such a hour as this—when both our hearts are bleeding so, and—and every breath we draw is like a curse upon us—it doesn't seem a fit time for us—for us to ——" The voice faltered and broke, leaving the speech unfinished.

Aunt Em kept silence so long that we fancied this appeal, too, had failed. Then abruptly, and without moving her head, she dropped a few ungracious words as it were over her shoulder : " If I had anything special to say, most likely I'd say it," she remarked.

We could hear the sigh that Serena drew. She lifted her shawled head, and for a moment seemed as if about to turn. Then she changed her mind, apparently, for she took a step nearer to the other.

" See here, Emmeline," she said, in a more confident tone. " Nobody in the world knows better than I do how thoroughly good a woman you are, how you have done your duty, and more than your duty, by your parents and your brothers, and your little stepson. You have never spared yourself for them, day or night. I have said often to—to him who has gone—that I didn't believe there was anywhere on earth a worthier or more devoted woman than you, his sister. And—now that he is gone—and we are both more sisters than ever in affliction—why in Heaven's name should you behave like this to me ? "

Aunt Em spoke more readily this time. " I don't know as I've done anything to you," she said in defence. " I've just let you alone, that's all. An' that's doin' as I'd like to be done by."

Still she did not turn her head, or lift her steady gaze from those closed doors.

"Don't let us split words!" entreated the other, venturing a thin, white hand upon Aunt Em's shoulder. "That isn't the way we two ought to stand to each other. Why, you were friendly enough when I was here before. Can't it be the same again? What has happened to change it? Only to-day, on our way up here, I was speaking to your father about you, and my deep sympathy for you, and——"

Aunt Em wheeled like a flash. "Yes, 'n' what did *he* say? Come, don't make up anything! Out with it! What did he say?" She shook off the hand on her shoulder as she spoke.

Gesture and voice and frowning vigour of mien were all so imperative and rough that they seemed to bewilder Serena. She, too, had turned now, so that I could see her wan and delicate face, framed in the laced festoons of black, like the fabulous countenance of "The Lady Iñez" in my mother's "Album of Beauty." She bent her brows in hurried thought, and began stammering, "Well, he said—Let's see, he said——"

"Oh, yes!" broke in Aunt Em, with raucous irony. "I know well enough what he said! He said I was a good worker—that they'd never had to have a hired girl since I was big enough to wag a churn dash, an' they wouldn't known what

to do without me. I know all that; I've heard
it on an' off for twenty years. What I'd like to
hear is, did he tell you that he went down South
to bring back *your* husband, an' that he never so
much as give a thought to fetchin' *my* husband,
who was just as good a soldier and died just as
bravely as yours did? I'd like to know—did he
tell you that.

What could Serena do but shake her head, and
bow it in silence before this bitter gale of words?

" An' tell me this, too," Aunt Em went on, lifting her harsh voice mercilessly, " when you was
settin' there in church this forenoon, with the
soldiers out, an' the bells tollin' an' all that—did
he say ' This is some for Alvy, an' some for Abel,
who went to the war together, an' was killed
together, or within a month o' one another?'
Did he say that, or look for one solitary minute
as if he thought it? I'll bet he didn't!"

Serena's head sank lower still, and she put up,
in a blinded sort of a way, a little white handkerchief to her eyes. " But why blame *me?* " she
asked.

Aunt Em heard her own voice so seldom that
the sound of it now seemed to intoxicate her.
" No! " she shouted. " It's like the Bible. One
was taken an' the other left. It was always Alvy
this an' Alvy that, nothin' for anyone but Alvy.
That was all right; nobody complained: prob'ly

he deserved it all ; at any rate, we didn't begrudge him any of it, while he was livin'. But there ought to be a limit somewhere. When a man's dead, he's pretty much about on an equality with other dead men, one would think. But it ain't so. One man gets hunted after, when he's shot, an' there's a hundred dollars for embalmin' him, an' a journey after him, an' bringin' him home, an' two big funerals, an' crape for his widow that'd stand by itself. The *other* man—he can lay where he fell ! Them that's lookin' for the first one are right close by—it ain't more'n a few miles from the Wilderness to Cold Harbour, so Hi Tuckerman tells me, 'an he was all over the ground two years ago—but nobody looks for this other man ! Oh, no ! Nobody so much as remembers to think of him ! They ain't no hundred dollars, no, not so much as fifty cents, for embalmin' *him*! No—*he* could be shovelled in anywhere, or maybe burned up when the woods got on fire that night, the night of the sixth. They ain't no funeral for him—no bells tolled—unless it may be a cow-bell up in the pasture that he hammered out himself. An' *his* widow can go around, week days an' Sundays, in her old calico dresses. Nobody ever mentions the word 'mournin' crape' to her, or asks her if she'd like to put on black. I 'spose they thought if they gave me the money for some mournin' I'd buy *candy* with it instead !"

With this climax of flaming sarcasm Aunt Em stopped, her eyes aglow, her thick breast heaving in a flurry of breathlessness. She had never talked so much or so fast before in her life. She swung the empty tin-pail now defiantly at her side to hide the fact that her arms were shaking with excitement. Every instant it looked as if she was going to begin again.

Serena had taken the handkerchief down from her eyes and held her arms stiff and straight by her side. Her chin seemed to have grown longer or to be thrust forward more. When she spoke it was in a colder voice—almost mincing in the way it cut off the words.

" All this is not my doing," she said. " I am to blame for nothing of it. As I tried to tell you, I sympathise deeply with your grief. But grief ought to make people at least fair, even if it cannot make them gentle and soften their hearts. I shall trouble you with no more offers of friendship. I—I think I will go back to the house now—to my little girl."

Even as she spoke, there came from the direction of the red barn a shrill, creaking noise which we all knew. At the sound Marcellus and I stood up, and Serena forgot her intention to go away. The barn doors, yelping as they moved on their dry rollers, had been pushed wide open.

## IV

THE first one to emerge from the barn was Hi
Tuckerman.   He started to make for the house,
but when he caught sight of our group, came
running towards us at the top of his speed,
uttering incoherent shouts as he advanced, and
waving his arms excitedly.   It was apparent that
something out of the ordinary had happened.

We were but little the wiser as to this something, when Hi had come to a halt before us, and
was pouring out a volley of explanations, accom-
panied by earnest grimaces and strenuous gestures.
Even Marcellus could make next to nothing of
what he was trying to convey, but Aunt Em,
strangely enough, seemed to understand him.
Still slightly trembling, and with a little occasional
catch in her breath, she bent an intent scrutiny
upon Hi, and nodded comprehendingly from time
to time, with encouraging exclamations, " He did,
eh ! "   " Is that so ? " and " I expected as much."
Listening and watching, I formed the uncharitable
conviction that she did not really understand Hi
at all, but was only pretending to do so in order
further to harrow Serena's feelings.

Doubtless I was wrong, for presently she
turned, with an effort, to her sister-in-law, and

remarked : " P'rhaps you don't quite follow what he's sayin' ? "

" Not a word ! " said Serena, eagerly. " Tell me, please, Emmeline ! "

Aunt Em seemed to hesitate. " He was shot through the mouth at Gaines' Mills, you know— that's right near Cold Harbour and—the Wilderness," she said, obviously making talk.

" That isn't what he's saying," broke in Serena. " What *is* it, Emmeline ? "

" Well," rejoined the other, after an instant's pause, " if you want to know—he says that ain't Alvy at all that they've got there in the barn."

Serena turned swiftly, so that we could not see her face.

" He says it's some strange man," continued Em, " a yaller-headed man, all packed an' stuffed with charcoal, so't his own mother wouldn't know him. Who it is nobody knows, but it ain't Alvy."

" They're a pack of robbers 'n' swindlers ! " cried old Arphaxed, shaking his long grey beard with wrath.

He had come up without our noticing his approach, so rapt had been our absorption in the strange discovery reported by Hi Tuckerman. Behind him straggled the boys and the hired men, whom Si Hummaston had scurried across from the house to join. No one said anything now, but tacitly deferred to the old man's principal right to speak. It was a relief to hear that terrible silence of his broken at all.

"They ought to all be hung!" he cried, in a voice to which the excess of passion over physical strength gave a melancholy quaver. "I paid 'em what they asked—they took a hundred dollars o' my money—an' they ain't sent me *him* at all! There I went, at my age, all through the Wilderness, almost clear to Cold Harbour, an' that, too, gittin' up from a sick bed in Washington, and then huntin' for the box at New York an' Albany, an' all the way back, an' holdin' a funeral over it only this very day—an' here it ain't *him* at all! I'll have the law on 'em though, if it costs the last cent I've got in the world!"

Poor old man! These weeks of crushing grief and strain had fairly broken him down. We listened to his fierce outpourings with sympathetic silence, almost thankful that he had left strength and vitality enough still to get angry and shout. He had been always a hard and gusty man; we felt by instinct, I suppose, that his best chance of weathering this terrible month of calamity was to batter his way furiously through it, in a rage with everything and everybody.

"If there's any justice in the land," put in Si Hummaston, "you'd ought to get your hundred dollars back. I shouldn't wonder if you could, too, if you sued 'em afore a Jestice that was a friend of yours."

"Why, the man's a fool!" burst forth Arphaxed, turning towards him with a snort. "I don't want the hundred dollars—I wouldn't 'a' begrudged a thousand—if only they'd dealt honestly by me. I paid 'em their own figure, without beatin' 'em down a penny. If it 'd be'n double, I'd 'a' paid it. What *I* wanted was *my boy*! It ain't so much their cheatin' *me* I mind, either, if it 'd be'n about anything else. But to think of Alvy—*my boy*— after all the trouble I took, an' the journey, an' my sickness there among strangers—to think that after it all he's buried down there, no one knows where, p'raps in some trench with private soldiers, shovelled in anyhow—Oh-h! they ought to be hung!"

The two women had stood motionless, with their gaze on the grass ; Aunt Em lifted her head at this.

"If a place is good enough for private soldiers to be buried in," she said vehemently, "it's good enough for the best man in the army. On Resurrection Day, do you think them with shoulder-straps 'll be called fust an' given all the front places ? I reckon the men that carried a musket are every whit as good, there in the trench, as them that wore swords. They gave their lives as much as the others did, an' the best man that ever stepped couldn't do no more."

Old Arphaxed bent upon her a long look, which had in it much surprise and some elements of menace. Reflection seemed, however, to make him think better of an attack on Aunt Em. He went on, instead, with rambling exclamations to his auditors at large.

" Makin' me the butt of the whole county ! " he cried. " There was that funeral to-day—with a parade an' a choir of music an' so on—an' now it 'll come out in the papers that it wasn't Alvy at all I brought back with me, but only some perfect stranger—by what you can make out from his clothes, not even an officer at all. I tell you the War's a jedgment on this country for its wickedness, for its cheatin' an' robbin' of honest men ! They wa'n't no sense in that battle at Cold Harbour anyway—everybody admits that ! —it was murder an' massacre in cold blood ;— fifty thousand men mowed down, an' nothin' gained by it !—an' then not even to git my boy's dead body back ! I say hangin's too good for 'em ! "

" Yes, father," said Myron, soothingly ; " but do you stick to what you said about the—the box ? Wouldn't it look better——"

" *No!* " shouted Arphaxed, with emphasis.

" Let Dana do what I told him—take it down this very night to the poor-master, an' let him bury it where he likes. It's no affair of mine. I wash my hands of it. There won't be no funeral held here ! "

It was then that Serena spoke. Strangely enough, old Arphaxed had not seemed to notice her presence in our group, and his jaw visibly dropped as he beheld her now standing before him. He made ·a gesture signifying his disturbance at finding her among his hearers, and would have spoken, but she held up her hand.

" Yes, I heard it all," she said, in answer to his deprecatory movement. " I am glad I did. It has given me time to get over the shock of learning—our mistake—and it gives me the chance now to say something which I—I feel keenly. The poor man you have brought home was, you say, a private soldier. Well, isn't this a good time to remember that there was a private soldier who went out from this farm—belonging right to this family—and who, as a private, laid down his life as nobly as General Sedgwick or General Wadsworth, or even our dear Alva, or any one else ? I never met Emmeline's husband, but Alva liked him, and spoke to me often of him. Men who fall in the ranks don't get identified, or brought home, but they deserve funerals as much as the others—just as much. Now this is my idea—let us feel that the mistake which has brought this poor stranger to us is God's way of giving us a chance to remember and do honour to Abel Jones. Let him be buried in the family lot up yonder, where we had thought to lay Alva, and let us do it reverently, in the name of Emmeline's husband, and of all others who have fought and died for our country—and with sympathy in our hearts for the women who, somewhere in the North, are mourning, just as we mourn here, for the stranger there in the red barn."

Arphaxed had watched her intently. He nodded now, and blinked at the moisture gathering in his old eyes. " I could e'en a'most 'a' thought it was Alvy talkin'," was what he said. Then he turned abruptly, but we all knew, without further words, that what Serena had suggested was to be done.

The men-folk, wondering doubtless much among themselves, moved slowly off toward the house or the cow-barns, leaving the two women alone. A minute of silence passed, before we saw Serena creep gently up to Aunt Em's side, and lay the thin white hand again upon her shoulder. This time it was not shaken off, but stretched itself forward, little by little, until its palm rested against Aunt Em's further cheek. We heard the tin-pail fall resonantly against the stones under the rail-fence, and there was a confused move-

ment as if the two women were somehow melting
into one.

"Come on, Sid!" said Marcellus Jones to me
"let's start them cows along.   If there's anything
I hate to see it's women cryin' on each other's
necks."

# THE EVE OF THE FOURTH

# THE EVE OF THE FOURTH

IT was well on toward evening before this Third of July all at once made itself gloriously different from other days in my mind.

There was a very long afternoon, I remember, hot and overcast, with continual threats of rain which never came to anything. The other boys were too excited about the morrow to care for present play. They sat instead along the edge of the broad platform-stoop in front of Delos Ingersoll's grocery-store, their brown feet swinging at varying heights above the sidewalk, and bragged about the manner in which they contemplated celebrating the anniversary of their Independence. Most of the elder lads were very independent indeed ; they were already secure in the parental permission to stay up all night, so that the Fourth might be ushered in with its full quota of ceremonial. The smaller urchins pretended that they also had this permission, or were sure of getting it. Little Denny Cregan attracted admiring attention by vowing that he should remain out, even if his father chased him with a policeman all around the ward, and he had to go and live in a cave in the gulf until he was grown up.

My inferiority to these companions of mine depressed me. They were allowed to go without shoes and stockings; they wore loose and comfortable old clothes, and were under no responsibility to keep them dry or clean or whole; they had their pockets literally bulging now with all sorts of portentous engines of noise and racket—huge brown "double enders," bound with waxed cord; long, slim, vicious-looking " nigger-chasers"; big " Union torpedoes," covered with clay, which made a report like a horse pistol, and were invaluable for frightening farmers' horses;—and so on through an extended catalogue of recondite and sinister explosives upon which I looked with awe, as their owners from time to time exhibited them with the proud simplicity of those accustomed to greatness. Several of these boys also possessed toy cannons, which would be brought forth at twilight. They spoke firmly of ramming them to the muzzle with grass, to produce a greater noise—even if it burst them and killed everybody.

By comparison, my lot was one of abasement. I was a solitary child, and a victim to conven-

tions. A blue necktie was daily pinned under
my Byron collar, and there were gilt buttons on
my zouave jacket. When we were away in the
pasture playground near the gulf, and I ventured
to take off my foot-gear, every dry old thistle-
point in the whole territory seemed to arrange
itself to be stepped upon by my whitened and
tender soles. I could not swim, so, while my lithe
bold comrades dived out of sight under the deep
water, and darted about chasing one another far
beyond their depth, I paddled ignobly around the
" baby-hole " close to the bank, in the warm and
muddy shallows.

Especially apparent was my state of humiliation on this July afternoon. I had no " double-
enders," nor might hope for any. The mere
thought of a private cannon seemed monstrous and
unnatural to me. By some unknown process of
reasoning my mother had years before reached
the theory that a good boy ought to have two ten-
cent packs of small fire-crackers on the Fourth of
July. Four or five succeeding anniversaries had
hardened this theory into an orthodox tenet of
faith, with all its observances rigidly fixed. The
fire-crackers were bought for me overnight, and
placed on the hall table. Beside them lay a long
rod of punk. When I hastened down and out in
the morning, with these ceremonial implements in
my hands, the hired-girl would give me, in an old

kettle, some embers from the wood-fire in the summer kitchen. Thus furnished, I went into the front yard, and in solemn solitude fired off these crackers one by one. Those which, by reason of having lost their tails, were only fit for " fizzes," I saved till after breakfast. With the exhaustion of these, I fell reluctantly back upon the public for entertainment. I could see the soldiers, hear the band and the oration, and in the evening, if it didn't rain, enjoy the fireworks; but my own contribution to the patriotic noise was always over before the breakfast-dishes had been washed.

My mother scorned the little paper torpedoes as flippant and wasteful things. You merely threw one of them, and it went off, she said, and there you were. I don't know that I ever grasped this objection in its entirety, but it impressed my whole childhood with its unanswerableness. Years and years afterward, when my own children asked for torpedoes, I found myself unconsciously advising against them on quite the maternal lines. Nor was it easy to budge the good lady from her position on the great two-packs issue. I seem to recall having successfully undermined it once or twice, but two was the rule. When I called her attention to the fact that our neighbour, Tom Hemingway, thought nothing of exploding a whole pack at a time inside their wash-boiler, she was not dazzled, but only replied: " Wilful waste makes woeful want."

Of course the idea of the Hemingways ever knowing what want meant was absurd. They lived a dozen doors or so from us, in a big white house with stately white columns rising from verandah to gable across the whole front, and a large garden, flowers and shrubs in front, fruit trees and vegetables behind. Squire Hemmingway was the most important man in our part of the town. I know now that he was never anything more than United States Comm issioner of Deeds, but in those days, when he walked down the street with his gold-headed cane, his blanket-shawl folded over his arm, and his severe, dignified, close-shaven face held well up in the air, I seemed to behold a companion of Presidents.

This great man had two sons. The elder of them, De Witt Hemingway, was a man grown, and was at the front. I had seen him march away, over a year before, with a bright drawn sword, at the side of his company. The other son, Tom, was my senior by only a twelvemonth. He was by nature proud, but often consented to consort with me when the selection of other available associates was at low ebb.

It was to this Tom that I listened with most envious eagerness, in front of the grocery-store, on the afternoon of which I speak. He did not

sit on the stoop with the others—no one expected
quite that degree of condescension—but leaned
nonchalantly against a post, whittling out a new
ramrod for his cannon.  He said that this year
he was not going to have any ordinary fire-
crackers at all ; they, he added with a meaning
glance at me, were only fit for girls.  He might
do a little in " double-enders," but his real point
would be in " ringers "— an incredible giant
variety of cracker, Turkey-red like the other, but
in size almost a rolling-pin.  Some of these he
would fire off singly—between volleys from his
cannon.  But a good many he intended to ex-
plode, in bunches say of six, inside the tin wash-
boiler, brought out into the middle of the road for
that purpose.  It would doubtless blow the old
thing sky-high, but that didn't matter.  They
could get a new one.

Even as he spoke, the big bell in the tower of
the town-hall burst forth in a loud clangour of
swift-repeated strokes.  It was half a mile away,
but the moist air brought the urgent, clamorous
sounds to our ears as if the belfry had stood close
above us.  We sprang off the stoop and stood
poised, waiting to hear the number of the ward
struck, and ready to scamper off on the instant
if the fire was anywhere in our part of the town.
But the excited peal went on and on, without a
pause.  It became obvious that this meant some-

thing beside a fire. Perhaps some of us wondered vaguely what that something might be, but as a body our interest had lapsed. Billy Norris, who was the son of poor parents, but could whip even Tom Hemingway, said he had been told that the German boys on the other side of the gulf were coming over to " rush " us on the following day, and that we ought all to collect nails to fire at them from our cannon. This we pledged ourselves to do—the bell keeping up its throbbing tumult ceaselessly.

Suddenly we saw the familiar figure of Johnson running up the street toward us. What his first name was I never knew. To every one, little or big, he was just Johnson. He and his family had moved into our town after the War began ; I fancy they moved away again before it ended. I do not even know what he did for a living. But he seemed always drunk, always turbulently good-natured, and always shouting out the news at the top of his lungs. I cannot pretend to guess how he found out everything as he did, or why, having found it out, he straightway rushed homeward, scattering the intelligence as he ran. Most probably Johnson was moulded by Nature for a town-crier, but was born by accident some generations after the race of bellmen had disappeared. Our neighbourhood did not like him ; our mothers did not know Mrs. Johnson, and we boys behaved with snobbish roughness to his children. He seemed not to mind this at all, but came up unwearyingly to shout out the tidings of the day for our benefit.

"Vicksburg's fell! Vicksburg fell!" was what we heard him yelling, as he approached.

Delos Ingersoll and his hired-boy ran out of the grocery. Doors opened along the street and heads were thrust inquiringly out.

"Vicksburg's fell!" he kept hoarsely proclaiming, his arms waving in the air, as he staggered along at a dogtrot past us, and went into the saloon next to the grocery.

I cannot say how definite an idea these tidings conveyed to our boyish minds. I have a notion that at the time I assumed that Vicksburg had something to do with Gettysburg, where I knew from the talk of my elders that an awful fight had been proceeding since the middle of the week. Doubtless this confusion was aided by the fact that an hour or so later on that same wonderful day, the wire brought us word that this terrible battle on Pennsylvanian soil had at last taken the form of a Union victory. It is difficult now to see how we could have known both these things on the Third of July—that is to say, before the people actually concerned seem to have been sure of them. Perhaps it was only inspired guesswork, but I know that my town went wild over the news, and that the clouds overhead cleared away as if by magic.

The sun did well to spread that summer-sky at eventide with all the pageantry of colour the spectrum knows. It would have been preposterous that such a day should slink off in dull, quaker drabs. Men were shouting in the streets now. The old cannon left over from the Mexican war had been dragged out onto the ricketty covered river-bridge, and was frightening the fishes, and shaking the dry, worm-eaten rafters, as fast as the swab and rammer could work. Our town bandsmen were playing as they had never played before, down in the square in front of the post-office. The management of the Universe could not hurl enough wild fireworks into the exultant sunset to fit our mood.

The very air was filled with the scent of triumph—the spirit of conquest. It seemed only natural that I should march off to my mother and quite collectedly tell her that I desired to stay out all night with the other boys. I had never dreamed of daring to prefer such a request in other years. Now I was scarcely conscious of surprise when she gave her permission, adding with a smile that I would be glad enough to come in and go to bed before half the night was over.

I steeled my heart after supper with the proud

resolve that if the night turned out to be as protracted as one of those Lapland winter nights
we read about in the geography, I still would not
surrender.

The boys outside were not so excited over the
tidings of my unlooked-for victory as I had expected them to be. They received the news, in
fact, with a rather mortifying stoicism. Tom
Hemingway, however, took enough interest in
the affair to suggest that, instead of spending my
twenty cents in paltry fire-crackers, I might go
down-town and buy another can of powder for
his cannon. By doing so, he pointed out, I would
be a part-proprietor, as it were, of the night's
performance, and would be entitled to occasionally
touch the cannon off. This generosity affected
me, and I hastened down the long hill-street
to show myself worthy of it, repeating the
instruction of " Kentucky Bear-Hunter-coarse-
grain " over and over again to myself as I
went.

Half-way on my journey I overtook a person
whom, even in the gathering twilight, I recognised as Miss Stratford, the school-teacher. She
also was walking down the hill, and rapidly. It
did not need the sight of a letter in her hand to
tell me that she was going to the post-office. In
those cruel war-days everybody went to the post-
office. I myself went regularly to get our mail,

and to exchange shin-plasters for one-cent stamps with which to buy yeast and other commodities that called for minute fractional currency.

Although I was very fond of Miss Stratford— I still recall her gentle eyes, and pretty, rounded, dark face, in its frame of long, black curls, with tender liking—I now coldly resolved to hurry past, pretending not to know her. It was a mean thing to do ; Miss Stratford had always been good to me, shining in that respect in brilliant contrast to my other teachers, whom I hated bitterly. Still, the " Kentucky Bear-Hun-ter-coarse-grain " was too important a matter to wait upon any mere female friendships, and I quickened my pace into a trot, hoping to scurry by unrecognised.

" O Andrew ! is that you ? " I heard her call out as I ran past. For the instant I thought of rushing on, quite as if I had not heard. Then I stopped, and walked beside her.

" I am going to stay up all night ; mother says I may ; and I am going to fire off Tom Heming-way's big cannon every fourth time, straight through till breakfast-time," I announced to her, loftily.

" Dear me ! I ought to be proud to be seen walking with such an important citizen," she answered, with kindly playfulness. She added more gravely, after a moment's pause : " Then

Tom is out, playing with the other boys, is
he ? "

"Why, of course!" I responded. "He always
lets us stand round when he fires off his cannon.
He's got some ' ringers ' this year, too."

I heard Miss Stratford murmur an impulsive
" Thank God ! " under her breath.

Full as the day had been of surprises, I could
not help wondering that the fact of Tom's ringers
should stir up such profound emotions in the
teacher's breast. Since the subject so interested
her, I went on with a long catalogue of Tom's
other pyrotechnic possessions, and from that to
an account of his almost supernatural collection
of postage stamps. In a few minutes more I am
sure I should have revealed to her the great secret
of my life, which was my determination, in case
I came to assume the victorious rôle and rank of
Napoleon, to immediately make Tom a Marshal
of the Empire.

But we had reached the post-office square. I
had never before seen it so full of people.

Even to my boyish eyes the tragic line of
division which cleft this crowd in twain was
apparent. On one side, over by the Seminary,
the youngsters had lighted a bonfire, and were
running about it—some of the bolder ones jump-
ing through it in frolicsome recklessness. Close
by stood the band, now valiantly thumping out

" John Brown's Body " upon the noisy night air. It was quite dark by this time, but the musicians knew the tune by heart. So did the throng about them, and sang it with lusty fervour. The doors of the saloon toward the corner of the square were flung wide open. Two black streams of men kept in motion under the radiance of the big reflector-lamp over these doors—one going in, one coming out. They slapped one another on the back as they passed, with exultant screams and shouts. Every once in a while, when move- ment was for the instant blocked, some voice lifted above the others would begin " Hip-hip- hip-hip—" and then would come a roar that fairly drowned the music.

On the post-office side of the square there was no bonfire. No one raised a cheer. A densely packed mass of men and women stood in front of the big square stone-building, with its closed doors, and curtained windows upon which, from time to time, the shadow of some passing clerk, bare-headed and hurried, would be momentariiy thrown. They waited in silence for the night- mail to be sorted. If they spoke to one another, it was in whispers—as if they had been standing with uncovered heads at a funeral service in a graveyard. The dim light reflected over from the bonfire, or down from the shaded windows of the post-office, showed solemn, hard-lined, anxious faces. Their lips scarcely moved when they muttered little low-toned remarks to their neighbours. They spoke from the side of the mouth, and only on one subject.

" He went all through Fredericksburg without a scratch———"

" He looks so much like me—General Palmer told my brother he'd have known his hide in a tan-yard———"

" He's been gone—let's see—it was a year some time last April———"

" He was counting on a furlough the first of this month—I suppose nobody got one as things turned out———"

" He said, ' No ; it ain't my style. I'll fight as much as you like, but I won't be nigger-waiter for no man, captain or no captain'———"

Thus I heard the scattered murmurs among the grown-up heads above me, as we pushed into the outskirts of the throng, and stood there, waiting with the rest. There was no sentence without a " he " in it. A stranger might have fancied that they were all talking of one man. I knew better. They were the fathers and mothers, the sisters, brothers, wives of the men whose regiments had been in that horrible three days' fight at Gettysburg. Each was thinking and speaking of his own, and took it for granted the others would understand. For that matter, they all did understand. The town knew the name and family of every one of the twelve-score sons she had in this battle.

It is not very clear to me now why people all went to the post-office to wait for the evening papers that came in from the nearest big city. Nowadays they would be brought in bulk and sold on the street before the mail-bags had reached the post-office. Apparently, that had not yet been thought of in our slow old town.

The band across the square had started up afresh with " Annie Lisle "—the sweet old refrain of " Wave willows, murmur waters " comes back. to me now after a quarter-century of forgetfulness, —when all at once there was a sharp forward movement of the crowd. The doors had been thrown open, and the hallway was on the instant filled with a swarming multitude. The band had stopped as suddenly as it began, and no more cheering was heard. We could see whole troops of dark forms scudding toward us from the other side of the square.

" Run in for me—that's a good boy—ask for Dr. Stratford's mail," the teacher whispered, bending over me.

It seemed an age before I finally got back to her, with the paper in its postmarked wrapper buttoned up inside my jacket. I had never been in so fierce and determined a crowd before, and I emerged from it at last, confused in wits and panting for breath. I was still looking about through the gloom in a foolish way for Miss Stratford, when I felt her hand laid sharply on my shoulder.

"Well—where is it ?—did nothing come ?" she asked, her voice trembling with eagerness, and the eyes which I had thought so soft and dove-like flashing down upon me as if she were Miss Pritchard, and I had been caught chewing gum in school.

I drew the paper out from under my round-about, and gave it to her. She grasped it, and thrust a finger under the cover to tear it off. Then she hesitated for a moment, and looked about her. "Come where there is some light," she said, and started up the street. Although she seemed to have spoken more to herself than to me, I followed her in silence, close to her side.

For a long way the sidewalk in front of every lighted store-window was thronged with a group of people clustered tight about some one who had a paper, and was reading from it aloud. Beside broken snatches of this monologue, we caught, now groans of sorrow and horror, now exclamations of proud approval, and even the beginnings of cheers, broken in upon by a general "'Sh-h !" as we hurried past outside the kerb.

It was under a lamp in the little park nearly half-way up the hill that Miss Stratford stopped, and spread the paper open. I see her still, white-faced, under the flickering gaslight, her black curls making a strange dark bar between the pale-straw hat and the white of her shoulder-shawl and muslin dress, her hands trembling as they held up the extended sheet. She scanned the columns swiftly, skimmingly for a time, as I could see by the way she moved her round chin up and down. Then she came to a part which called for closer reading. The paper shook perceptibly now, as she bent her eyes upon it. Then all at once it fell from her hands, and without a sound she walked away.

I picked the paper up, and followed her along the gravelled path. It was like pursuing a ghost, so weirdly white did her summer attire now look to my frightened eyes, with such a swift and deathly silence did she move. The path upon which we were, described a circle touching the four sides of the square. She did not quit it when the intersection with our street was reached, but followed straight round again toward the point where we had entered the park. This, too, in turn she passed, gliding noiselessly forward under the black arches of the overhanging elms. The suggestion that she did not know she was

going round and round in a ring startled my
brain. I would have run up to her now if I had
dared.

Suddenly she turned, and saw that I was behind
her. She sank slowly into one of the garden-
seats, by the path, and held out for a moment a
hesitating hand toward me. I went up at this
and looked into her face. Shadowed as it was,
the change I saw there chilled my blood. It was
like the face of some one I had never seen
'̀ore, with fixed, wide-open, staring eyes
;h seemed to look beyond me through the
darkness, upon some terrible sight no other
could see.

" Go—run and tell—Tom—to go home !
His brother—his brother has been killed," she
said to me, choking over the words as if they
hurt her throat, and still with the same strange
dry-eyed, far-away gaze covering yet not seeing
me.

I held out the paper for her to take, but she
made no sign, and I gingerly laid it on the seat
beside her. I hung about for a minute or two
longer, imagining that she might have something
else to say—but no word came. Then, with a
feebly inopportune "Well, good-bye," I started off
alone up the hill.

It was a distinct relief to find that my companions were congregated at the lower end of the

common, instead of their accustomed haunt
further up near my home, for the walk had been
a lonely one, and I was deeply depressed by what
had happened.   Tom, it seems, had been called
away some quarter of an hour before.   All the
boys knew of the calamity which had befallen the
Hemingways.   We talked about it from time to
time, as we loaded and fired the cannon which
Tom had obligingly turned over to my friends.
It had been out of deference to the feelings of the
stricken household that they had betaken themselves and their racket off to the remote corner ⟨⟩
the common.   The solemnity of the occasion silenced criticism upon my conduct in forgetting to
buy the powder.   " There would be enough as long
as it lasted," Billy Norris said, with philosophic
decision.

We speculated upon the likelihood of De Witt
Hemingway being given a military funeral,
These mournful pageants had by ⟨t⟩is time
become such familiar things to us that the prospect of one more had no element of excitement
in it, save as it involved a gloomy sort of
distinction for Tom.   He would ride in the first
mourning-carriage with his parents, and this would
associate us, as we walked along ahead of the
band, with the most intimate aspects of the
demonstration.   We regretted now that the
soldier-company which we had so long projected

remained still unorganised. Had it been other-wise we would probably have been awarded the right of the line in the procession. Some one suggested that it was not too late—and we promptly bound ourselves to meet after breakfast next day to organise and begin drilling. If we worked at this night and day, and our parents instantaneously provided us with uniforms and guns, we should be in time. It was also arranged that we should be called the De Witt C. Heming-way Fire Zouaves, and that Billy Norris should be side-captain. The chief command would, of course, be reserved for Tom. We would specially salute him as he rode past in the closed carriage and then fall in behind, forming his honorary escort.

None of us had known the dead officer closely, owing to his advanced age. He was seven or eight years older than even Tom. But the more elderly among our group had seen him play base ball in the academy nine, and our neighbourhood was still alive with legends of his early audacity and skill in collecting barrels and dry-goods boxes at night for election bonfires. It was remembered that once he carried away a whole front-stoop from the house of a little German tailor on one of the back streets. As we stood around the heated cannon, in the great black solitude of the common, our fancies pictured this redoubtable young man once more among us—not in his blue uniform, with crimson sash and sword laid by his side, and the gauntlets drawn over his lifeless hands, but as a taller and glorified Tom, in a roundabout jacket and copper-toed boots, giving the law on this his playground. The very cannon at our feet had once been his. The night air became peopled with ghosts of his contemporaries—handsome boys who had grown up before us, and had gone away to lay down their lives in far-off Virginia or Tennessee.

These heroic shades brought drowsiness in their train. We lapsed into long silences, punctuated by yawns, when it was not our turn to ram and touch off the cannon. Finally some of us stretched ourselves out on the grass, in the warm darkness, to wait comfortably for this turn to come.

What did come instead was daybreak—finding Billy Norris and myself alone constant to our all-night vow. We sat up and shivered as we rubbed our eyes. The morning air had a chilling freshness that went to my bones—and these, moreover, were filled with those novel aches and stiffnesses which beds were invented to prevent. We stood up, stretching out our arms, and gaping at the pearl-and-rose beginnings of the sunrise in the eastern sky. The other boys had all gone home, and taken the cannon with them. Only scraps of torn paper and tiny patches of burnt grass marked the site of our celebration.

My first weak impulse was to march home without delay, and get into bed as quickly as might be. But Billy Norris looked so finely resolute and resourceful that I hesitated to suggest this, and said nothing, leaving the initiative to him. One could see, by the most casual glance, that he was superior to mere considerations of unseasonableness in hours. I remembered now that he was one of that remarkable body of boys, the paper-carriers, who rose when all others were asleep in their warm nests, and trudged about long before breakfast distributing the *Clarion* among the well-to-do households. This fact had given him his position in our neighbourhood as quite the next in leadership to Tom Hemingway.

He presently outlined his plans to me, after having tried the centre of light on the horizon, where soon the sun would be, by an old brass compass he had in his pocket—a process which enabled him, he said, to tell pretty well what time it was. The paper wouldn't be out for nearly two hours yet—and if it were not for the fact of a great battle there would have been no paper at all on this glorious anniversary—but he thought we would go down-town and see what was going on around about the newspaper office. Forthwith we started. He cheered my faint spirits by assuring me that I would soon cease to be sleepy, and would, in fact, feel better than usual. I dragged my feet along at his side, waiting for this revival to come, and meantime furtively yawning against my sleeve.

Billy seemed to have dreamed a good deal, during our nap on the common, about the De Witt C. Hemingway Fire Zouaves. At least he had now in his head a marvellously elaborated system of organisation, which he unfolded as we went along. I felt that I had never before realised his greatness, his born genius for command. His scheme halted no where. He allotted offices with discriminating firmness ; he treated the question of uniforms and guns as a trivial detail which would settle itself ; he spoke with calm confidence of our offering our services to the Republic in the autumn ; his clear vision saw even the materials for a fife-and-drum corps among the German boys in the back streets. It was true that I appeared personally to play a meagre part in these great projects : the most that was said about me was that I might make a fair third-corporal. But Fate had thrown in my way such a wonderful chance of becoming intimate with Billy, that I made sure I should swiftly advance in rank— the more so as I discerned in the background of his thoughts, as it were, a grim determination to make short work of Tom Hemingway's

aristocratic pretensions, once the funeral was
over.

We were forced to make a detour of the park
on our way down, because Billy observed some
half-dozen Irish boys at play with a cannon inside, whom we knew to be hostile.   If there had
been only four, he said, he would have gone in
and routed them.   He could whip any two of
them, he added, with one hand tied behind his
back.   I listened with admiration.   Billy was not
tall, but he possessed great thickness of chest and
length of arm.   His skin was so dark that we
canvassed the theory from time to time of his
having Indian blood.   He did not discourage this,
and he admitted himself that he was double-
jointed.

The streets of the business-part of the town
into which we now made our way, were quite deserted.   We went around into the yard behind the
printing-office, where the carrier-boys were wont
to wait for the press to get to work ; and Billy
displayed some impatience at discovering that
here too there was no one.   It was now broad
daylight, but through the windows of the com-
posing-room we could see some of the printers,
still setting type by kerosene lamps.

We seated ourselves at the end of the yard on
a big, flat, smooth-faced stone, and Billy produced
from his pocket a number of " m " quads, he

called them, with which the carriers had learned
from the printers' boys to play a very beautiful
game. You shook the pieces of metal in your
hands, and threw them on the stone ; your score
depended upon the number of nicked sides that
were turned uppermost. We played this game in
the interest of good-fellowship for a little. Then
Billy told me that the carriers always played it for
pennies—and that it was unmanly for us to do
otherwise. He had no pennies at that precise
moment, but would pay at the end of the week
what he had lost ; in the meantime there was my
twenty cents to go on with. After this Billy
threw so many nicks uppermost that my
courage gave way, and I made an attempt to
stop the game ; but a single remark from him
as to the military destiny which he was reserv-
ing for me if I only displayed true soldierly
nerve and grit, sufficed to quiet me once more,
and the play went on. I had now only five
cents left.

Suddenly a shadow interposed itself between
the sunlight and the stone. I looked up, to behold a small boy with bare arms and a blackened
apron standing over me, watching our game.
There was a great deal of ink on his face and
hands, and a hardened, not to say rakish, expression in his eye.

" Why don't you 'jeff' with somebody of your

own size?" he demanded of Billy, after having looked me over critically.

He was not nearly so big as Billy, and I expected to see the latter instantly rise and crush him, but Billy only laughed and said we were playing for fun ; he was going to give me all my money back. I was rejoiced to hear this, but still felt surprised at the propitiatory manner Billy adopted toward this diminutive inky boy. It was not the demeanour befitting a side-captain —and what made it worse was that the strange boy loftily declined to be cajoled by it. He sniffed when Billy told him about the military company we were forming ; he coldly shook his head, with a curt " nixie ! " when invited to join it ; and he laughed aloud at hearing the name our organisation was to bear.

" He ain't dead at all—that De Witt Hemingway," he said, with jeering contempt.

" Hain't he though ! " exclaimed Billy. " The news come last night. Tom had to go home— his mother sent for him—on account of it ! "

" I'll bet you a quarter he ain't dead," responded the practical inky boy. " Money up, though ! "

" I've only got fifteen cents. I'll bet you that, though," rejoined Billy, producing my torn and dishevelled shin-plasters.

" All right ! wait here ! " said the boy, running

off to the building and disappearing through the
door. There was barely time for me to learn
from my companion that this printer's-apprentice
was called "the devil," and could not only whistle
between his teeth and crack his fingers but
chew tobacco, when he reappeared, with a long
narrow strip of paper in his hand. This he held
out for us to see, indicating with an ebon forefinger the special paragraph we were to read.
Billy looked at it sharply, for several moments,
in silence. Then he said to me : "What does it
say there ? I must 'a' got some powder in my
eyes last night."

I read this paragraph aloud, not without an
unworthy feeling that the inky boy would now
respect me deeply :

"CORRECTION. Lieutenant De Witt C. Hemingway, of Company A, —th New York, reported
in earlier despatches among the killed, is uninjured.
The officer killed is Lieutenant Carl Heinninge,
Company F, same regiment."

Billy's face visibly lengthened as I read this
out, and he felt us both looking at him. He
made a pretence of examining the slip of paper
again, but in a half-hearted way. Then he rue-
fully handed over the fifteen cents, and, rising
from the stone, shook himself.

" Them Dutchmen never was no good!" was what he said.

The inky boy had put the money in the pocket under his apron, and grinned now with as much enjoyment as dignity would permit him to show. He did not seem to mind any longer the original source of his winnings, and it was apparent that I could not with decency recall it to him. Some odd impulse prompted me, however, to ask him if I might have the paper he had in his hand. He was magnanimous enough to present me with the proofsheet on the spot. Then with another grin he turned and left us.

Billy stood sullenly kicking with his bare toes into a sand-heap by the stone. He would not answer me when I spoke to him. It flashed across my perceptive faculties that he was not such a great man, after all, as I had imagined. In another instant or two it had become quite clear to me that I had no admiration for him whatever. Without a word, I turned on my heel and walked determinedly out of the yard and into the street, homeward bent.

All at once I quickened my pace ; something had occurred to me. The purpose thus conceived grew so swiftly that soon I found myself running. Up the hill I sped, and straight through the park. If the Irish boys shouted after me I knew it not, but dashed on heedless of all else save the one idea. I only halted, breathless and panting, when I stood on Dr. Stratford's doorstep, and heard the night-bell inside jangling shrilly in response to my excited pull.

As I waited, I pictured to myself the old doctor as he would presently come down, half-dressed and pulling on his coat as he advanced. He would ask eagerly, " Who is sick ?   Where am I to go ? " and I would calmly reply that he unduly alarmed himself, and that I had a message for his daughter. He would, of course, ask me what it was, and I, politely but firmly, would decline to explain to any one but the lady in person.   Just what might ensue was not clear— but I beheld myself throughout commanding the situation, at once benevolent, polished, and in-exorable.

The door opened with unlooked-for prompt-ness, while my self-complacent vision still hung in mid-air.   Instead of the bald and spectacled old doctor, there confronted me a white-faced, solemn-eyed lady in a black dress, whom I did not seem to know.   I stared at her, tongue-tied, till she said, in a low, grave voice : " Well, Andrew, what is it ? "

Then of course I saw that it was Miss Stratford, my teacher, the person whom I had come to see. Some vague sense of what the sleepless night had meant in this house came to me as I gazed con-

Q

fusedly at her mourning, and heard the echo of her sad tones in her ears.

"Is some one ill?" she asked again.

"No; some one—some one is very well!" I managed to reply, lifting my eyes again to her wan face. The spectacle of its drawn lines and pallor all at once assailed my wearied and over-taxed nerves with crushing weight. I felt myself beginning to whimper, and rushing tears scalded my eyes. Something inside my breast seemed to be dragging me down through the stoop.

I have now only the recollection of Miss Stratford's kneeling by my side, with a supporting arm around me, and of her thus unrolling and reading the proof-paper I had in my hand. We were in the hall now, instead of on the stoop, and there was a long silence. Then she put her head on my shoulder and wept. I could hear and feel her sobs as if they were my own.

"I—I didn't think you'd cry—that you'd be so sorry," I heard myself saying, at last, in de-spondent self-defence.

Miss Stratford lifted her head, and, still kneel-ing as she was, put a finger under my chin to make me look her in her face. Lo! the eyes were laughing through their tears; the whole countenance was radiant once more with the light of happy youth, and with that other glory which youth knows only once.